The Last Red Cent

David Fetter

The Last Red Cent

HuBBuB Books
Norman, Oklahoma

Published by HuBBuB Books, LLC, Norman, Oklahoma

Cover and Interior Design: David Fetter
Editing: Terry Best
Proofing: Cindy Fetter

Fetter, David, 1959 -

The Last Red Cent

Library of Congress Control Number: 2018902076

ISBN: 978-0-9997326-0-1

1. Fiction 2. Western

Sharps 50-90 Rifle - Wikimedia I, Arthurrh [GFDL (http://www.gnu.org/copyleft/fdl.html), CC-BY-SA-3.0 (http://creativecommons.org/licenses/by-sa/3.0/) or CC BY-SA 2.5-2.0-1.0 (https://creativecommons.org/licenses/by-sa/2.5-2.0-1.0)], via Wikimedia Commons

Indian Head Penny - Wikipedia By US Mint (coin), National Numismatic Collection (photograph by Jaclyn Nash) [Public domain or Public domain], via Wikimedia Commons

Train - McCammon Idaho 1882 public domain photo taken prior to 1920

Back Cover Silhouette and Sun - David Fetter

For My Father-In-Law, Bill Storm,
Who Wears A White Hat

1

Spilled ink ran across the tiny desk.

The black viscous fluid flowed toward the open ledger threatening to drown the rows of neat numbers arrayed across the lined beige paper.

Leon stood and quickly lifted the account book above the desk.

"Tarnation," he hissed under his breath. He inhaled quickly to stifle any further curses and to lessen his mostly forgotten Alabama drawl.

The clerk set the ledger on his chair and dabbed at the ink with an old blackened rag. He blew on the desktop to dry the ink stain before putting the ledger back. A second rag was used to wipe his shaking hands, and then he threw the dirty tatters into a basket under his desk.

Leon warily looked around the room. Row after row of identical men in white shirts and dark trousers pored over ledgers propped on small desks. Some tallied deliveries of gold bullion while others calculated the corresponding output of blanks and newly minted coins. Weights and values, values and weights. Everything accounted for. Nothing left to chance.

He looked up at the clock. A few minutes till six. Soon, he thought, another workday finishes and another whiskey-soaked evening begins. His stomach grumbled, and he wiped beads of sweat from his forehead. He leaned forward and his shirt followed, clinging to his back.

✳✳✳

The accounts manager took the ledger from Leon and marked it on his worksheet as having been returned. Leon turned toward the exit licking his cracked lips. He looked forward to that first drink.

"Hey, Leon. Come back here."

Leon froze in place.

"You forgot to sign out for your ledger."

Leon's tensed muscles relaxed as fear flowed out of his body and relief washed over his face.

"Sorry, sir. I guess I just wasn't thinking."

Leon smiled and signed the space next to his employee number.

A few minutes later he emerged onto Fifth Street outside the imposing San Francisco Federal Mint. The sounds and smells of the busy city reverberated off of the sturdy granite foundation and basement of the fortress only to be soaked up by the porous sandstone upper floors.

Since the end of the War Between North and South, the entire country, or at least the part that hadn't worn the gray uniforms of the Confederacy, had undergone a boom the likes of which no one had previously seen, and now The *Granite Lady* held no less than one-third of the growing U.S. gold reserves.

Leon stopped at a tobacconist's shop to purchase a plug of tobacco and scanned the street to make sure that he wasn't being followed. He chose a circuitous route heading southwest into the Mission District. After traveling for about thirty minutes, he walked slowly, but deliberately, past an upholsterer's shop and paused in the doorway of a saloon situated in the corner of a faded red, clapboard three-story building. Leon entered the open doorway and journeyed from daylight to near blackness.

He squinted his eyes and struggled to make out the interior of the small tavern. Two tired-looking men in dirty, threadbare clothes leaned against the bar, each staring into a glass, and each strategically stationed next to a stained and dented spittoon. They served as a warning to Leon of what he could become.

Leon squinted harder, and a lone small table appeared like an apparition in the back of the bar. A heavy man in a too-small hat sat in one chair. An empty chair sat next to him and, glowing like a beacon at sea, a full bottle and two glasses sat upon the table. The man beckoned to Leon and Leon warily walked over to the table.

He sat and silently studied his contact, whom everyone referred to as simply, 'The Fat Man'.

The Fat Man slid the bottle over to Leon.

"Howdy do," said Leon, as he poured himself a glass from the bottle.

"Howdy do, Private. You got something for me?"

The Fat Man pushed five coins across the table. Leon quickly pocketed the money and guzzled the whiskey that he had just poured.

Leon's worried face relaxed as he began to pour himself another drink.

"I surely do, Sarge."

The Fat Man glared at Leon. He grabbed the bottle around the neck and held tight. The knuckles on his plump hand turned white, shaking from exertion and anger.

"Major," hissed The Fat Man. "I'm a major in the Army of the Confederacy, and I'll receive the respect due a line officer. Don't you ever forget that, Private!"

Leon fixed his eyes on the bottle that now lay firmly in the clutches of the man seated across from him. It was plain as day that to play along with him was the smartest plan.

"Beg your pardon...," the slightest of pauses, and then Leon finished, "Major. I thought it best not to use any distinguishing language, lest anyone should overhear our conversation."

Leon looked him straight in the eyes to show his sincerity.

True enough, he thought, The Fat Man had been a major at one point—even if his daddy did buy his commission. That is, before he'd been court-martialed for gross incompetence for leading his men into certain death. To top it off, The Fat Man had galloped away in sheer terror when his men needed him most.

Leon remembered that General Armistead had wanted to put The Fat Man in front of a firing squad, but The Fat Man's family had intervened, so they court martialed him, took away his commission, and made him a sergeant. The other men didn't want anything to do with him, so they moved him to the death detail where he couldn't harm the living. It was there, however, that The Fat Man learned to strip the dead of any valuables and their last shreds of dignity. From there he had made his way to the Confederate prison camp at Andersonville, Georgia where he served as personal assistant to the commandant, Captain Henry Wirz.

Wirz had been captured and held at the Old Capitol Prison in Washington D.C. and later hanged for war crimes. In the end, he had paid for his sins; but somehow

The Fat Man had managed to escape justice—and here he was, in the flesh, sitting across the table, sharing a drink.

Leon shivered at the thought of The Fat Man having the power of life and death over a helpless prisoner. Sometimes the perversity of life floored him.

With his free hand, The Fat Man reached into his jacket pocket and pulled out a pearl handled snub-nose revolver. He set it on the table in front of him.

Leon looked with dread at the pistol. He looked around the saloon to see if anyone was watching them.

"Don't you think you should put that away?" said Leon. I don't think you'll be needin' that in here. No one followed me."

"It's a beauty, ain't it?" said The Fat Man. "A .44 caliber Bulldog revolver, just like the one that Charles Guiteau used to assassinate President Garfield. He did us all a great service by shooting that bastard. First Lincoln, now Garfield."

The Fat Man smiled. "Mark my words Private, he won't be the last Yankee tyrant to fall from an assassin's bullet. This accursed Union cannot stand."

Another Reb who would not or could not let go of the war—the *Great Lost Cause*, Leon thought. Precisely the reason that he had come to California and San Francisco—to lose himself in a land new enough that it lacked the old tired memories.

Unfortunately, the old didn't loosen its grip so easily. The proof was sitting right in front of him.

"Someday," Leon whispered to himself. He smiled at The Fat Man and cleared his throat.

"Major," said Leon, "I got somethin' you'll want to hear, sir."

The Fat Man loosened his grip on the bottle and relaxed.

The crisis averted, Leon and The Fat Man leaned closer together as the whiskey coursed through Leon's brain and released his tongue's grip on his dormant southern accent. Lazy, meandering words snaked into barely whispered sentences.

"I done like you said, Major. I found a man on the shippin' dock that was real down on his luck and I took him boozin' and whorin'. Told him I might be able to slip some coins his way for a little information 'bout the where to and what for of any large shipments goin' out from the mint."

"And what did you find out?"

"Big shipment headin' out to Tucson the twenty-third July on the Southern Pacific."

"How big?"

"My friend says he reckons at least eighty thousand in gold coins and bank notes. Maybe more. Some of it headed for the bank there in Tucson and the rest to go further on to El Paso."

The Fat Man tipped his hat back on his head and let out a soft whistle.

"You sure, eighty-thousand? How many guards?"

"Maybe two. He wasn't sure," said Leon. "Ridin' in the express car."

The Fat Man finished his drink and slowly stood up. In the process, his considerable stomach bumped the table. The whiskey bottle teetered, and, fearing catastrophe, Leon sprang into action to steady the container and its precious contents.

"You've done good, Private. Something extra. Keep up the good work."

He slid another coin over to Leon and brushed past him.

Leon watched The Fat Man slowly walk from the bar into the dimming daylight. He poured another drink and let the liquor's warmth wash over him.

Turning in his chair, he looked back at the bar.

The drunk closest to the table raised his gaze from his glass and took in the saloon. He walked to the table and sat in the chair that had previously been occupied by The Fat Man.

"Howdy, Captain," said Leon.

"Howdy, Private," replied the man across the table.

"What have you got to report?" he asked as he slid a small pile of bills toward Leon.

***

Kirby Barksdale stepped onto the rickety porch of the Picacho way station. He was a big man, north of six foot and heavy in the saddle—heavy even for his big black stallion. The dry boards groaned under his boots as he pulled open the battered door. Inside the one-room cabin, a table and four chairs sat next to a dented, tobacco-stained potbelly stove. Shelves of dry goods and sundries lined one wall. A narrow, scuffed and scarred wooden counter stood in front of the shelves.

The gnarled, old stationmaster behind the counter nursed a lukewarm cup of coffee and perused a month-old copy of the Tucson newspaper. When he saw Kirby—whom he knew as Roy—he beamed from ear to ear, revealing a picket of yellowed teeth that populated his mouth like old tombstones in a long-neglected graveyard.

"Howdy, Roy. You come in to replenish your supplies? Can I pour you a cup?"

"Got anything stronger?" asked Kirby.

"Well, of course I do," said the stationmaster.

He pulled a bottle from under the counter and poured some whisky into a dirty glass. Kirby threw a coin onto the counter and picked up the drink.

"Got a letter for ya," said the stationmaster.

"Ya got a sweetheart, Roy? Says it come all the way from San Francisco, from a Nellie Taylor."

He handed the letter to Kirby who tore open the envelope and sat down at the table.

"Naw," said Kirby, "Nellie's my niece."

Kirby sipped his whisky and slowly read the letter.

After a minute, he smiled and drummed out a happy rhythm on the table.

"Good news?" asked the stationmaster.

"Nothin' but," said Kirby. "Nothin' but."

"Well then, how about another drink, Roy?"

"I think I will. I feel like a bit of celebratin'."

"What's the good news?"

"Well now, it seems that my family is marryin' into money."

"Why, that's real nice, Roy. Nellie marryin' a rich beau? San Francisco family you say? Is they old money?"

"Nope, new money for sure."

The stationmaster rubbed his chin and poured a little rye into his coffee cup.

Kirby put the letter back into the envelope and tucked it into his shirt pocket. He rose from the table and walked over to the counter with his empty glass, holding it out for a refill.

"On the house," said the old man, as he poured Kirby's drink.

The stationmaster paused mid-pour and said to Kirby,

"Say Roy, you goin' to the wedding?"

"Yep."

"Ya goin' all the way to San Francisco, huh?"

"Nope."

"Well, how you gonna see the wedding then?"

"Oh, I'm goin' all right. Nellie and her rich fiancé are comin' to Tucson by train."

"Big wedding? I mean, this feller being rich and all."

"Yep. There'll be a whole trainload of guests," said Kirby.

Kirby smiled at the old man and added, "'Course I'll be there and a few of my closest friends."

He set his empty glass on the counter.

"Well, thanks for the company. Best be movin' on. Lots to do before the wedding."

"All right then, Roy. Be seein' ya around."

Kirby turned and crossed the floor of the small train station in a few long strides. A quick flash of bright sunlight announced the opening and closing of the door, and Kirby was gone.

The old man returned to his newspaper.

"Young love", he mumbled to himself. "Bet ol' Roy'll find a way to get some of that *new money* tucked into his saddle bags."

The Fat Man shifted his considerable weight. The seats in the train were made for much thinner passengers, and he longed for the thick upholstered sofas in the San Francisco whorehouse that he frequented.

His clothes stuck to his body, and he felt as if he were melting. He had discarded his jacket, shirt collar, and hat fairly quickly, but propriety kept him from further undress.

With each passing day since leaving San Francisco, it was, as if, the train got a little bit closer to hell. Now, somewhere between Sweetwater and Casa Grande, The Fat Man took solace that this infernal journey would soon be coming to an end.

He wiggled his toes and attempted to paddle his ten little piggies in the sweat that pooled in his boots. Intolerable and vexing, he thought. A man of his standing and family bearing shouldn't be expected to venture into this hellhole. Still, it seemed that to get his share of the money he would be required to travel to Tucson.

Kirby had been adamant about that—a final test of loyalty before Kirby paid him his share.

Posing as a lawyer on business, the plan was to witness the holdup. Then, in Tucson, it would be his job to muddy the waters as much as he could concerning the details of the robbery and the men who had committed it. After talking to the sheriff, his next stop would be the saloon where he would relate the false details of the robbery to anyone who would listen.

The Fat Man glanced around the car at the other passengers. Mostly women and older men, he observed. A mother and her two young children sat in the back of the train. One weathered cowboy slept at the front end of the car, his back against the wall and his hat pulled down over his eyes. This one might be trouble, thought The Fat Man.

Since leaving San Francisco, The Fat Man had changed trains four times and had seen passengers come and go—except for one man. He appeared to be in his fifties, dressed like a salesman with graying black hair. He was a quiet fellow who kept to himself, but was friendly with the porters and conductors. Probably traveled a lot and everyone knew him. He had boarded the first train out of San Francisco before The Fat Man got on. Come to think of it, he had always been the last to leave and the first to board whenever they changed trains. This man ate by himself and never seemed to talk to any of the other passengers. The Fat Man judged that the quiet man was most likely a peddler.

He didn't know why, but something about this traveler struck him as odd.

The Fat Man puzzled the significance of the mysterious passenger for another five minutes before resting his frazzled brain. He uncorked the bottle in his bag and downed a couple of large swigs of rye. It was not long before the whiskey, the heat, and the swaying of the train overpowered him, and he succumbed to sleep.

3

The first sign of trouble inside the passenger car was the squealing of the train's brakes. The cowboy sat up in his seat and straightened the hat on his head. He looked out the window and quickly pulled his head back into the car. The wind had blown off his Stetson and he mashed down the greasy hair on his now hatless head.

The train shuddered and came to a full stop.

"Looks like a holdup folks. Appears someone has loosened one of the tracks up ahead. I seen five men on horseback waiting for the train to come to a standstill."

An older man travelling with his wife stood up and approached the cowboy.

"Do you think we can keep these men at bay until help arrives? I've got a gun," he said as he patted his jacket.

"I'm not giving up my belongings without a fight," he continued.

The cowboy unbuckled his gun belt and set it on the floor of the car in the aisle.

"You do what you want old man. But I'm not risking my life for a few dollars and some old pocket watches. Those men don't look like they're foolin' around."

The mother pulled her children up close to her, one under each arm.

Mumbling could be heard throughout the car as the passengers debated what to do.

The quiet salesman stood and held up his hands.

"Listen, folks, listen up!"

The passengers continued to talk among themselves.

"Listen up, please. I'm afraid he's right. Those men are outlaws, and we're no match for them."

The passengers stopped talking, and all eyes were on the once quiet man.

"The best possible outcome is for all of us to travel on to Tucson unharmed, and the only way that's going to happen is if we do as we're told and don't do anything stupid."

"Now if you have a gun," he continued, "I suggest that you do as this man did and put it on the floor in plain sight. Chances are that one or two of these men will board the train and insist on taking your valuables. Give them whatever they want with no fuss and no guff. Remember, they're just looking for an excuse to get rough."

The Fat Man smiled at the sensible speech that poured out of the salesman's mouth.

This would be easy, he thought.

"They'll be boarding any minute," the quiet man said. "Go ahead and put your hands in the air to put them at ease."

The quiet man was clearly now in charge. Everyone raised their hands and waited.

★★★

It had taken a while for the train to come to a complete stop. Kirby sat high in his saddle watching for any signs of resistance from the passengers or crew. He breathed in the scent of coal smoke, grease, and horse sweat from behind his bandana. A small bead of perspiration rolled down from his forehead to his brow, but quickly evaporated in the arid desert heat.

The rest of the gang sat atop their mounts dividing their attention between the stationary locomotive and Kirby. Two of the outlaws scanned the engine with rifles in case the crew decided to put up a fight. They were five men total, each eager for his share of some easy money. All were seasoned bandits except one, but all were willing to break the law and risk gunshot or hanging.

A gloved hand waved a white cloth from the engine compartment.

"Engineer's givin' up, Kirby," said the bandit to Kirby's left.

"Yeah, I can see that. Keep those rifles ready."

Kirby lifted the bottom of his bandana away from his chin and spit tobacco juice onto the ground.

"Danny, you and Levi get up there and get them men outta the locomotive and down on the ground where we can keep an eye on 'em."

The two outlaws rode forward, pistols drawn. Danny rode straight ahead covering the right side of the train and Levi crossed in front of the engine to cover the left side.

"Get on down from there," Danny shouted at the engineer and the stoker.

The pot-bellied engineer carefully climbed down to the ground. He moved a few steps away from the train, and the young rail-thin stoker jumped to the ground beside him.

Danny steadied his pistol at the two railroad men.

"Levi, you climb on up there and take a look. Make sure there ain't no one lingerin' behind."

Levi climbed up the steps on the left side of the engine, pistol still drawn.

"All clear," shouted Levi.

Danny waved the other outlaws forward. The five men formed a semi-circle around the engineer and stoker.

"How many others on board who're working for the railroad?" Kirby asked the engineer.

The engineer peered up at Kirby and squinting at the bright sun, said, "Conductor's in the passenger car. We ain't got no caboose on this run."

"What about the mail car?" asked Kirby.

"I don't know. That car's been locked since I took over this run yesterday."

"What's it carryin'?" Kirby asked the engineer.

The engineer swallowed hard before answering, "I don't know that either, I swear to God mister."

Danny cleared his throat and said, "Well then, in your experience, how many's likely to be in there?"

Kirby glared at Danny and said, "I'll do the askin'."

"Okay, answer up then. How many you think are in that mail car?"

The engineer looked back and forth from Danny to Kirby before addressing Kirby.

"Depends on what it's carryin'. If it's just mail, then maybe nobody. They lock up the doors and then unlock 'em when it gets to where it's goin'."

The engineer looked up at Danny and continued, "If it's somethin' else worth guardin'—well then, two, maybe three men will ride along."

The engineer paused, and then continued, "Like I said, though, car's been locked since I took over. Ain't seen no one come or go."

"Guess we'll just have to take a look then," said Kirby.

***

The conductor ran out the back of the passenger car.

"Stop, stay here with us," the salesman yelled to the fleeing conductor. A masked horseman galloped by on one side of the passenger car, his pistol drawn.

A single shot rang out while simultaneously three more outlaws rode fast on the other side of the train.

One man boarded from the front of the car and the outlaw who had galloped after the conductor boarded from the back. Both men wore bandanas over their faces and pulled their hats low on their foreheads. Each pointed a pistol at the passengers. The man in the front held a large muslin bag in one hand.

"What a pretty sight," said the bandit at the rear of the car.

The Fat Man stole a glance to the rear and recognized the outlaw as Walt Henderson. He identified him by the x-shaped scar on Walt's forehead and his bright green eyes. He didn't know the younger boy at the front of the car. Walt was fearless, but reckless, thought The Fat Man.

"If you don't want to end up like the conductor, then I suggest you stay put. You've been real sensible so far, so let's keep it that way."

The old man who was facing the front of the car turned to look at the outlaw in the back who was doing all the talking.

"Did you kill the conductor?" he asked.

"He shouldn't have run off," said Walt.

"Turn back around. Keep your eyes straight ahead and nobody move."

The old man did as he was told.

"We don't want to hurt no one, but we will if we have

to. You folks are small potatoes. We got bigger fish to fry."

The Fat Man grimaced. What a stupid thing to say, he thought. The Fat Man felt uneasy and glanced at the salesman. He was watching him. He was sure of it.

"So, here's what we're gonna do. My partner is gonna walk on down the aisle like a pretty little bride and he's gonna ask each of you to stand one at a time. He's gonna pat you down for weapons and then he's gonna ask you to empty out your pockets and put anything of value into that bag. Next, you're gonna open up your luggage and let him have a peek inside. He tells you to take anything out, you do it and put it in the bag."

The outlaw at the front was silent. He was short and stood about five foot five in his boots. Sandy hair spilled from beneath his stained hat and light brown peach fuzz peeked out from the top of the bandana covering his lower face. The young outlaw's unblinking gaze darted around the passenger car. His nervous eyes finally fixed upon the other outlaw at the back of the car.

On a signal from Walt, the young outlaw moved up the aisle of the train and held out the dirty cloth bag to each passenger in turn. The bag began to fill up with belongings.

The Fat Man watched as the young outlaw held out the bag to the salesman who silently dropped a pocket watch and a wallet and chain into the sack.

"Them glasses, too," said the young bandit who pointed at the eyeglasses that peeked out from the salesman's vest pocket.

"Surely, you can leave a man his reading glasses, son."

A voice from the rear of the car responded, "Leave him his glasses. We don't need 'em, Bobby."

The young outlaw squinted at the mention of his name.

"Okay, now your luggage," he said.

The salesman stood, took down his trunk and set it on the seat.

"Open it."

The quiet man did as he was told, revealing a trunkful of Bibles.

"Why all the Bibles?" asked Bobby.

"I peddle them. I'm a Bible salesman."

Bobby thumbed through the pages of the Bibles that were stacked on top, and then lifted them up to see more Bibles neatly stacked to the bottom of the trunk.

"Leave him his Bibles," said the outlaw at the back of the car.

The salesman closed the trunk and placed it back overhead. He sat down in his seat and looked into Bobby's eyes.

The young outlaw averted the salesman's gaze and moved across the aisle to The Fat Man who reached into the jacket lying on the seat and put his empty wallet into the bag.

"Turn the jacket pockets inside out," said Bobby.

"But there isn't anything else in there," said The Fat Man.

"Just do it," said the other outlaw from the back of the car.

The Fat Man sulkily turned out the pockets revealing his Webley revolver.

"Real gentle now," said Bobby. "Put it in the bag."

"Hold up there," said Walt.

He strode up beside The Fat Man and savagely backhanded him across the cheek.

"You can't do that to me," The Fat Man protested. He stared at Walt in disbelief.

"That's for lyin'" said the outlaw. "Gimme that gun, Bobby."

Bobby handed the revolver to the older outlaw who tucked it into his belt.

He walked back to the rear of the train and continued his supervision of Bobby's work.

"Open your luggage, mister."

The Fat Man stood and pulled down his suitcase. He opened it revealing a half-empty bottle of whiskey.

Bobby held up the bottle for the other outlaw's inspection.

"Put it in the bag," said Walt from the rear of the car.

"You can't take that," said The Fat Man. "I need that to steady my nerves. I've got a condition."

"Drink some milk, it'll help you sleep," said Walt. "Now shut up or I'll shut you up."

The Fat Man leaned back in his seat and said nothing, glaring at Bobby like a petulant child.

So, thought The Fat Man, Kirby hadn't told Bobby that he was in on the robbery. Walt, though, was clearly having fun at his expense. He made a mental note to himself to retrieve his pistol and whiskey—and to give Kirby a piece of his mind for subjecting him to such humiliation.

He looked straight ahead as Bobby methodically proceeded to the rear of the train collecting the passengers' valuables.

Out of the corner of his eye, The Fat Man perceived that the Bible salesman was watching him.

Something about this man isn't right, he thought—he 's too sure of himself, too poised, too calm. Disquiet began to gnaw at The Fat Man's mind.

A quick look would tell him if the Bible salesman was indeed watching him.

The Fat Man turned his head and glanced at the quiet man.

The salesman was looking straight ahead, his eyes studying the front of the passenger car.

Thank God, thought The Fat Man. Nothing to worry about.

But then, the quiet man slowly turned his head toward The Fat Man. They locked eyes and the quiet man acknowledged The Fat Man with an almost imperceptible smile.

The Fat Man's face turned ashen and his blood ran cold. Despite the heat, he began to shiver. He quickly turned away and looked down at the floor of the passenger car.

Jesus, he thought, he knows I'm in on it.

***

Danny had seen the conductor a split second before Walt bore down on the man and shot him in the back with a single round from his Smith and Wesson.

Well, that does it, Danny thought, now it's a hangin' offense for sure. Ain't gonna be no holdin' back now.

Walt let out a whoop and dismounted his moving horse. He headed toward the rear platform of the passenger car. Young Bobby Bristow, the newest member of the gang, had already entered the car from the front with pistol drawn. Bobby was to serve as the bagman gathering up the passengers' belongings while Walt stood back and watched over Bobby.

The frightened passengers watched as the three remaining horsemen galloped past on their way to the ultimate prize locked inside the express car that was hitched behind the passenger car and two freight cars.

The outlaws remained on their horses using the corner of the last freight car as cover. No movement was seen from the mail car. Kirby grabbed a Winchester '73 from the man beside him. He sidled his horse up a little closer to the corner of the freight car and raised the rifle.

"You, in there. Come on out now, and no one gets hurt. You waste our time and ya'll will be sorry."

Kirby's voice disappeared into the desert stillness.

He paused a few beats and then resumed, "We ain't foolin'. Ya'll will be in a world of hurt if ya don't open them doors and come on out. We got fire and dynamite. How'd ya rather die—burned up or blowed up. Take your pick."

More silence. "Dammit, open them doors," yelled Kirby.

The gang leader put three bullets into the mail car.

Danny glanced at Kirby who was becoming more enraged with each passing minute. He cupped his hands around his mouth to form a megaphone and said, "C'mon, we're gonna get in there in the end. We can rob you alive or we can rob you dead. Ain't no difference to us. But, the first way you get to go home and sleep in a bed, second way you get to sleep under a pile of dirt."

A pause to let the message sink in and then, "Amount they's payin' you can't be worth dyin' for. Be sensible."

Kirby raised his rifle. "They ain't comin' out, dammit."

Danny put his hand on Kirby's shoulder and said, "Hold up. Give 'em a minute to talk it over."

"You got one minute to think it through," Kirby yelled to the men inside the mail car.

"Get me that dynamite," Kirby said to the man whose rifle he had taken.

A voice from inside the mail car hollered out, "We're comin' out."

"All right then, get on out," said Kirby.

"But you got to promise you won't shoot us the minute we step outta the door."

Kirby contemplated the deal and then said, "Okay, you got my word."

The sound of a large metal bolt turning could be heard followed by the thud of a wooden beam being dropped to the floor. The large door to the mail car slowly slid open.

"Throw out your weapons," said Kirby.

Two rifles flew to the ground followed by three pistols still in their holsters and gun belts.

"Now jump on outta there."

The three men jumped to the ground with their hands raised. They blinked at the bright sunlight.

"Okay, now kneel down and put your hands behind your heads."

The guards did as they were told and Kirby said, "Levi, go check and see that there ain't no one hiding in that mail car. We'll cover you from here."

Levi dismounted his horse and warily made his way to the side of the mail car.

"Anybody else in there?" he asked the railroad men.

"Nobody, I swear to God," said the man who had done all of the talking.

"You better not be lyin," said Levi as he put his gun into his holster and in one swift movement pulled himself into the dark interior of the mail car.

A minute passed before Levi reappeared in the doorway.

"All clear," he yelled. "And there's a big 'ol safe in here!"

Kirby and Danny got off their mounts and quickly advanced to the mail car.

"What's the combination to that safe?" Kirby demanded of the guards.

"We don't know the combination," said the lead guard.

Kirby backhanded the guard with the barrel of his pistol and said, "You tell me the combination or you're all dead men. I'll shoot you one at a time until I open that safe."

"We can't open it," said the guard. "They change the combination at the bank and telegraph the new combination ahead to the next bank. The banker in Tucson has the combination now. After he gets the money for his bank, then he changes it and telegraphs the banker in El Paso."

The guard looked up at Danny and pleaded, "Don't kill us, please. I'd open that safe for you if I could."

Danny grabbed Kirby's wrist and said, "They're tellin' the truth Kirby. They're scared to death. If they knew the combination they'd be yellin' it to the heavens. Let's blow the safe with the TNT and get outta here."

"Right," said Kirby, "we finish this job and add it to the other money we already got and we'll be set for life. Let's get a move on."

Levi ran back to the horses and grabbed a saddlebag. He hustled back to the mail car and grinned at Kirby.

"Not too much, Levi," said Danny. "We came for gold coins, not gold dust. Remember last time."

Levi smiled, and said, "It's a mite bigger safe this time. Don't worry, I'll be gentle."

He hopped up into the mail car and said, "Ya'll need to get back some." He threw the saddlebag over one shoulder and disappeared into the blackness.

Kirby nudged the prisoners with his gun, steering them to a spot he judged to be a good distance from the mail car.

"Okay, lay on your bellies and put your hands behind your heads," he said.

Kirby and Danny turned their attention to the mail car where Levi appeared in the doorway carrying a spool of fuse, the now empty saddlebag over one shoulder. He turned to face the mail car and, walking backwards into the desert, began to unspool the fuse.

Suddenly a shot rang out, and Levi spun around before falling to the ground.

Kirby and Danny instinctively dropped to the ground.

"It come from that last freight car," said Danny.

All three men shot into the wooden siding of the freight car where the black barrel of a rifle could be seen through an open slat.

Two more shots rang out from the freight car, but were harmlessly swallowed up by the desert.

The outlaws fired again, narrowing in on the rifle.

The rifle suddenly swung up in the open slat and pointed skyward.

"You told me that there wasn't anyone else guarding that safe," Kirby yelled at the three railroad men who lay prone in the dirt.

"We didn't know he was in there," the guard whimpered. "He must of boarded sometime last night. It ain't our fault."

Levi slowly picked himself up and held his left arm.

Danny ran to Levi and said, "You okay, Levi?"

"Yeah, I think so. He just winged me."

As Danny advanced toward Levi, Kirby stood over the guards.

"Please mister, don't kill us. We didn't do nothin'. Have mercy on us, please."

"You don't deserve no mercy," Kirby said before he shot each of them.

＊＊＊

The passengers startled at the sound of the first rifle shot that boomed like a bass drum from outside the train. And then the fusillade of return fire and its accompanying thunderous cacophony caused some to cower down in fear and others to grab the backs of their heads and lean far forward in their seats.

The Fat Man stared apprehensively at the two outlaws at the back of the car who had just finished the task of robbing the passengers. The salesman unflinchingly watched The Fat Man.

The mother and her two children began to quietly weep setting off a chain reaction of soft wailing and moaning among not just the women, but several of the men.

"What the hell?" said Walt.

"Don't nobody move," he commanded.

Bobby looked at Walt and said, "What do you suppose happened?

"I don't know, but I aim to find out. They might need some help. You stay here and keep an eye on the passengers. Anybody moves, you shoot 'em. Understand?"

"Yep," said Bobby who surveyed the frightened passengers through wide eyes.

Walt turned and hurried out the back door in the direction of the gunfire.

Bobby felt alone and vulnerable as he struggled to stop the shaking that had started in his knees and had now made its way as far north as his gun hand.

Tarnation, thought Bobby, I want to be somewhere else—anywhere else but this damned train.

✳✳✳

Walt came running full-tilt around the corner of the freight car to see Kirby, pistol drawn, still standing over the three railroad men. He was cussing the dead men and kicking dirt onto the silent figures. Danny steadied Levi who nursed his arm. Both men stared in silence at the executioner and the executed lying in the desert sand.

"You okay?" Walt yelled to Levi.

Kirby spun around, his gun pointed at Walt.

"Whoa, whoa, hold up there Kirby. It's just me," said Walt.

Kirby angrily holstered his pistol and glared at Walt.

"Only winged me," Levi chuckled hoping to ease the tension.

"Well, let's get on with it. Sooner we get what's in that safe, the sooner we can get outta here," said Kirby who turned and walked away from the dead guards.

Walt and Levi joined him, while Danny finished spooling out the fuse. All of the men avoided looking at the dead men, except Kirby who kicked one of the bodies in the leg as he passed and mumbled, "You'd still be alive if you hadn't been so stupid."

"Ya'll ready?" asked Danny.

"Let's get 'er done," said Kirby and they all turned their backs on the mail car and crouched down. Danny cut the fuse from the spool, flicked a match, and touched it to the cut end.

The fuse fizzled and hissed at the outlaws like a scared snake, and the fire ran off toward the train.

Danny took a peek behind him and saw the fuse twizzle its way off the ground and climb into the darkened mail car.

"Fire in the hole," he yelled as he turned away.

The sound of the dynamite reverberated through the dry desert air and vibrated through the bodies of the four crouching men. Small pieces of wood floated down around them and settled on their hats and shoulders.

"Hot damn," shouted Levi when he saw the damage that his handiwork had done to the mail car. Most of the front of the car was gone and the roof had disappeared. The safe lay in the sand in front of the car.

"Damn you Levi, you better not have used too much of that dynamite," said Kirby.

They ran to the safe, which had landed on one of its sides, hinges up. The door was partially cracked next to the combination lock.

"C'mon boys, let's flip 'er to the other side so we can finish pryin' the door off," shouted Danny. "Get some of them crowbars from the saddle bags."

Walt and Levi soon returned with the crowbars, and they began working on the door while Kirby kicked at it with the heel of his boot.

Danny watched as the door began to move. Finally, it popped loose from the deadbolts. Kirby threw it open, and the four outlaws stared in disbelief.

Inside, stuffed to the gills, were bags and bags of coins and more bags of neatly banded bank notes.

"I never seen so much money in one place at one time," said Walt.

"How much ya reckon's there?" asked Levi.

"My contact says about eighty-thousand," said Kirby.

"It's more'n that," said Danny dreamily.

"Let's get this loaded up and get outta here," commanded Kirby. "There'll be time enough to count it when we get it back to the hideout."

"We got ten horses includin' the packhorses to load up," said Danny. "We'll fetch 'em while you stay here," Danny said to Kirby.

***

"I know you," said the salesman.

The Fat Man stared ahead trying desperately to ignore the quiet man.

"I know you," the salesman repeated.

The Fat Man turned his head toward the salesman. The smile remained on the quiet man's face and generated a feeling of friendliness, but when The Fat Man looked into his blue eyes the warm feeling was replaced with cold resolve and dread purpose.

"I don't believe we've met," The Fat Man curtly replied.

"I never said we'd met. I just said that I know you."

"I'm a lawyer from San Francisco, sir. Never been out this way. I don't believe I've ever had the pleasure of making your acquaintance," said The Fat Man.

"Oh, I know you all right," insisted the salesman. "In a previous life, maybe. You weren't a lawyer then."

"I don't see how that's possible, sir. I'm just a simple man who keeps to himself. I have business in Tucson."

"You're too modest. I know you by reputation," the quiet man replied.

An immense explosion rocked the passenger car and interrupted the conversation between the two men. In response, The Fat Man closed his eyes and covered his ears with his hands.

He opened his eyes to the sight of the salesman's weak smile and brutal gaze.

The passenger car filled with the noise of panic.

"Stay put and quiet down," Bobby yelled at the passengers.

"You see," continued the quiet man, "it's hard to forget a man of such renown—some would say notoriety."

Clearly irritated, The Fat Man shouted, "I tell you we don't know each other!"

The curious passengers directed their eyes at the two men, and Bobby said, "Shut up, you two. Quiet down or you'll regret it."

The passengers returned to fretting, and the salesman said in a quiet voice, "Care for a Bible," and after a slight pause, "Major? Or should I say…Sergeant?"

I don't know what you're talking about," said The Fat Man unsteadily.

"They say that scripture helps soothe a troubled soul. I think in your case, Psalm 25:11 would be appropriate. Do you know that verse, Major?"

The Fat Man looked at the salesman in terror.

"I can see by your face that it's unfamiliar to you. Let me refresh your memory."

The salesman moved a little closer to The Fat Man and recited in a measured voice, "For Your name's sake, O Lord, pardon my iniquity, for it is great."

The Fat Man began to sweat and fidget in his seat before he said, "Jesus speaks of love and forgiveness, sir. Would it do any good to ask forgiveness?"

"You can ask Jesus' forgiveness when you see him. He ain't on this train," said the salesman.

The Fat Man stood bolt upright and yelled to Bobby, "Boy, get on back here. I need to get off this train."

"Shut up mister and sit back down."

"I need to get off this train, right now," continued The

Fat Man. "I demand to speak to Kirby."

Bobby stared at The Fat Man and said, "How do you know that name, mister?"

"I just do. You need to keep a good eye on this one," said The Fat Man, pointing at the salesman.

The quiet man's smile got a little wider and he folded his arms.

Bobby walked to The Fat Man and pointed his gun at his chest.

"I don't know anybody named Kirby," said Bobby.

"Don't be stupid boy. I told you, I need to talk to Kirby now."

"Ya ain't gettin' off this train, so sit down and shut up."

The Fat Man pushed Bobby's head back with a quick palm to the boy's chin and simultaneously wrenched his gun hand backwards at the wrist, causing Bobby to loosen his grip on the pistol.

The Fat Man's unexpected agility and quickness took Bobby by surprise as he sailed backward over the seat behind him.

The gun skittered under the salesman's seat, and The Fat Man scooted into the aisle and ran to the back door and out of the train as quickly as his large frame permitted.

The quiet man reached under the seat and retrieved the pistol.

Bobby lay in the aisle and watched The Fat Man exit the passenger car. He frantically looked for his pistol under the seats.

"You lookin' for this?" said the salesman.

A look of horror washed over Bobby's face when he saw the pistol in the man's hand.

"Here, take it," said the quiet man, as he offered the

pistol to Bobby.

Bobby eyed the salesman with a mixture of bafflement and caution.

"Here, take it," he repeated. "You best be after him son, or there'll be hell to pay."

Bobby stood and took the pistol from the quiet man's outstretched hand.

Without so much as a thank you he ran out the rear door in pursuit of The Fat Man.

★★★

"Well, that's the last of it," said Danny.

He cinched the bulging saddlebag tight. The brown mare, visibly weighted down, stamped in protest.

"She don't like carryin' so much," said Danny. "Maybe we should've used a wagon."

"She ain't got no rider," said Kirby. "She can handle the load all right. 'Sides, a wagon just would've slowed us down."

"Best we get goin' then. No reason hangin' about," said Danny.

"Walt, you go round up Bobby. Let them passengers know what happens if anyone decides to play the hero," said Kirby.

Levi spun, drew his gun, and pointed it toward the freight car, alerting the others to do likewise. The four bandits faced the freight car, pistols drawn—all nerves and sinew.

The figure of The Fat Man waddled toward them noticeably upset and obviously out of breath.

"Kirby, Kirby Wheeler, you gotta take me with you," panted The Fat Man.

"Hold up, Major," shouted Kirby.

"Put me on one of them horses. We gotta get out of here, now," said The Fat Man.

"Damn fool," hissed Danny under his breath.

Kirby slowly walked toward The Fat Man who was doubled over, hands on his knees and winded from fear and exertion. "Why ain't you on that train? You shouldn't be out here. We agreed that you was to go on into Tucson to put the sheriff off the trail. Now everyone on that train knows that you're in on the holdup."

"You know him?" Levi asked Danny.

Danny didn't reply. He just stared at The Fat Man and shook his head in disbelief at The Fat Man's display of monumental stupidity.

"Yeah, we know him," Walt volunteered at Danny's silence. "Knew him from the war. He was a sneak and a coward then and just more of the same now."

"He's as good as dead to Kirby now," said Danny under his breath. "No way he's takin' him with us on one of them horses."

"Please take me with you," The Fat Man pleaded.

"We can't do that. No extra horses to pack you out of here," said Kirby.

"Well then, you can leave my share behind and give me one of the packhorses."

Kirby made a half-hearted laugh and then said, "Leave behind your share? Now I know you're crazy. We ain't leavin' behind anyone's share, you can count on that, Major."

"But, on the train, I seen..." said The Fat Man.

The outlaws watched as the figure of young Bobby ran into view.

"Hey, mister," Bobby yelled as he rounded the corner of the freight car. "I told you to stay put."

The Fat Man, surprised, spun to face Bobby. The outlaw leveled his pistol at him.

"Kirby, I told him to stay put, but he tricked me," said Bobby.

"Listen kid, I need you to shut up. I've got somethin' important to tell Kirby," said the The Fat Man.

"I told you to stay put on the train and I'm tellin' you to stay put now," said Bobby.

Angry, The Fat Man took a step forward. Bobby shot, and the bullet found its target in his ample chest.

Simultaneously, Kirby fired two rounds into The Fat Man's back. The Fat Man dropped to his knees and then fell forward.

Bobby ran to The Fat Man and stared at him as he lay face down in the dirt.

Kirby joined Bobby, and together they studied The Fat Man's body.

"I'm sorry, Kirby," said Bobby. "I told him to sit down and shut up, but he got the drop on me."

✷✷✷

My eyes don't seem to be working, thought Major Gerard Henri Toutant-Beauregard.

Major Gerard Henri Toutant-Beauregard.

He decided he would be known as Major G.H.T. Beauregard—he would use his initials in the fashion of his uncle, the illustrious General P.G.T. Beauregard.

He liked the sound of the military title in front of his name. It made him smile—or, it would have, had he been capable of forming a smile.

His face wasn't working either.

Just moments earlier, he had been so hot—now he was very cold.

Where was he?

Why, I'll ask someone where I am, thought the Major.

He tried to form his mouth into the shape of the word 'hello' and to move his tongue to the roof of his mouth.

Strange, now his mouth didn't seem to be working.

He remembered the first day that he had called himself, major.

His parents had been so proud of him when he had been commissioned an officer in the newly formed Confederate States Army. Father had thrown him a grand soirée, at which all of the best families of New Orleans had turned out. He had worn his uniform for the first time and had danced until he could no longer stand. Ah, the magical power of a uniform upon the female psyche was a wonder to behold—even the prettiest belles had danced with him that evening.

Happy days!

His uncle, who had wrangled the commission as a favor to the family, had been less so. He had taken him aside, and rather unkindly, had said, "Do not make me regret aiding you, nephew. If I am dishonored, embarrassed, or even inconvenienced by your conduct, then I will not come to your aid, nor will I hesitate to mete out the strictest of punishments.

"To this point you have proved to be nothing but a burden to your poor parents and a black mark upon your gender. I have always believed that a good dose of military discipline might make a man of you, and now that war is upon us, you may make amends for your previous very undistinguished existence."

Uncle Gustave certainly had been true to his word.

When his men had refused to follow his orders, and

had suffered grave casualties as a result, his uncle had done nothing to defend the family's honor. After all, it had hardly been his fault that his horse had bolted and could not be calmed until he had traveled five miles from the battle. When he had protested his unjust treatment at the hands of the court martial, his uncle had replied that he had done everything that could be done, and that he was lucky that he had escaped the gallows or a firing squad.

The Major heard himself snort and gurgle.

Nothing wrong with his ears, he thought.

He heard a man's voice. He recognized the voice. It was the scoundrel, Kirby Barksdale.

Something pinged in the dark recesses of his brain—this Kirby fellow owed him money. He would need to be stouthearted if he wanted to collect.

One must walk lightly with Kirby. He had a terrible temper.

The Major thought of the first time he had met Kirby.

It was following all of the indignities that had been visited upon him by the Army. First he had been court martialed, and then he had been stripped of his commission and had been reduced to the rank of sergeant.

The final affront had been assigning him to death and funeral duty—or so, they thought. Being the crafty fellow that he was, he had found a way to turn that to his advantage too.

It had turned out that many of the dead on both sides of the skirmishes carried with them small mementos and sundry tokens of home. Some of these were valuable enough to pilfer outright, while others served as useful clues leading to the names and addresses of the dead soldier's family and loved ones. A well-written letter to the poor boy's relatives often led to remuneration in exchange for the return of said mementos—or perhaps a lock of hair.

He had managed to turn a tidy profit from his funereal duties, but his greatest triumph was still to come.

Through good fortune, he had become acquainted with a group of soldiers who were being transferred to the Andersonville prisoner-of-war camp to serve as guards.

They spoke of all the money that they hoped to make on the side. He had engaged in a friendly poker game with the men and had convinced one of them to exchange duties in return for forgiving his gambling debt.

And so, he became a prison guard.

Prison duty had suited him, and through hard work, grit, and determination, he had risen to become the personal assistant to Captain Henry Wirz, the commandant of the prison.

One day, at the tail end of the war, they had brought in a Yankee lieutenant who had been caught in a raid in Northern Virginia. The lieutenant had insisted that he was not a Yankee, but rather a Confederate, who had disguised himself as a Yankee.

The lieutenant had been Kirby.

Barksdale had told the Major his tale of the train robbery and the hidden money, but the Major had not believed him—until a new guard had told the Major that he had served with Barksdale and that he most surely was not a Yankee, but rather, a deserter. It was only when the guard was brutally murdered, that the Major knew for sure that Kirby was telling the truth.

The two men had struck a bargain in the prison camp— the Major would facilitate Kirby's escape, and Kirby would reward him with a portion of the hidden money.

The only catch—there was always a catch with Kirby— had been that he must leave with Kirby, thereby making himself guilty of desertion and binding their fates.

He had thought long and hard about the bargain before following through. The consequences of getting caught would have been death, but in the end the siren call of the money had been too much.

So, he had hidden Kirby in a wagon and bribed two of the guards to let him pass without a customary search. When they had arrived at the destination that Kirby had specified, the Major was sure he would either be killed or left for dead. But, Kirby had been true to his word, and the Major was rewarded handsomely.

After the war, he had worked with Kirby as an advance man or gathering intelligence for jobs both large and small. And each time, Kirby would require some extra sign of loyalty from the Major—but without fail, he had always paid him.

Kirby had always been fair. But there was one thing that the Major had learned early on about Kirby—stick to the agreed-upon terms of the deal and steer clear of Kirby's temper—failure to do either could be deadly.

Yes sir, thought the Major, hitching his wagon to Kirby's star had proven a stroke of genius. He had done very well so far.

Now, about that money that Kirby owed him. He intended to collect if he could only make his legs work.

Why couldn't he move?

Maybe Kirby would be so kind as to help him to his share of the money?

***

Kirby shot another round into The Fat Man's body.

"Ain't no problem, kid. One less share to divvy up."

Kirby nudged The Fat Man with his foot, and judging the big man to be dead, said, "We been here long enough."

"You heard him," said Danny. "Let's mount up and get goin.'"

"What about the passengers?" asked Levi.

"Ain't none of them gonna be sorry when they see us leavin,'" said Walt. "I don't judge anyone on that train to have the backbone to try to stop us. Ain't that right, Bobby?"

Bobby glanced warily at Kirby and said nothing.

4

The passengers watched the outlaws as they rode off from the train—five men on horseback leading five spares, all heavy in the saddle.

"They're gettin' away," said the cowboy.

"How long until we can fix that track and get on to Tucson?" asked the old man.

"Best all you folks get to the far side of the car," the salesman said as he stood and retrieved his case from the overhead rack.

He opened the case and dumped out the Bibles. Reaching down into the empty case with both hands he pressed down on two of the corners at the same time, and the bottom of the case sprang up. The salesman removed the false bottom and examined the neatly arrayed large-caliber bullets.

He got down onto his hands and knees and reached up underneath his seat. A rifle dropped into his open palm.

The Bible salesman stood with the rifle and popped up the peep sight. The passengers gasped, and the cowboy moved to the opposite side of the car. The passengers took their cue from the cowboy and moved away.

The quiet man watched as the bandits trotted away in no particular hurry. Kirby, Walt and Levi led their packhorses and were already a considerable distance from the train. Bobby had had trouble securing his portion of the money to his horse and Danny had stayed behind to help

him get squared away. Now, they urged on their heavily
laden animals to catch up with the rest of the gang.

The cowboy watched the salesman reach into the suitcase and pull out one of the long deadly-looking bullets.

"Buffalo gun?" asked the cowboy.

"Shiloh Sharps," said the quiet man." He took his reading glasses out of his pocket and calmly put them on. "This
one ain't never seen a buffalo—only men."

He pushed the gun's lever forward to open the breach
on the rifle and loaded a bullet. The gun made a metallic
shh-took sound as the quiet man pulled the lever back. He
cocked the gun's hammer and studied the riders through
the window.

"Gettin' a mite far away, ain't they?" said the old man.
His wife shushed him.

The salesman peered over the top of his reading glasses
and wrapped his jacket around one of his hands that he
had balled into a fist. The two closest riders were now at
least a quarter mile away.

"Want 'em far enough away so they can't double back
on me before I get another round loaded," he replied, as
he broke out the window with his fist. He cleared the glass
from the frame and unwrapped the jacket from his hand.
The two closest riders stopped and turned at the sound of
the breaking glass.

The first rider wildly gesticulated to the rider in the rear
and shouted a panicked warning. Both riders turned and
made a run for it. The other three riders watched from
about a thousand yards farther away as their brethren sped
toward them as fast as their steeds could carry them.

The quiet man rested the rifle barrel on the windowsill
and took aim. He elevated the barrel a few degrees and

set the rear trigger. He exhaled and willed his body still.

The salesman barely brushed the front hair trigger and felt the kick of the rifle transmit to his shoulder and down to his gut. An ear-splitting crack reverberated through the passenger car.

"Sorry, kid," said the quiet man.

The passengers said nothing.

The heavy bullet caught the young bandit in the small of the back. His arms shot outward as if he were about to give someone a big hug, and then he pitched forward onto his horse's neck.

Miraculously, the horse galloped on with its dead rider bouncing in the saddle. Eventually, the jostling proved too violent and Bobby was thrown onto the sand and scrub. His horse, its bridle hanging to the ground, stopped and looked back at the motionless rider. The frightened pack horse galloped away from the shot.

✶✶✶

Danny held up a hundred yards farther away from where Bobby had fallen and looked back at the train. He could make out a long gun barrel sticking out of a window. He feared that he would be next and turned his horse to flee. A chorus of shouting arose from the other outlaws. Bobby's packhorse went racing past him in the direction of the waiting gang.

"Get the money, get the money," they yelled.

He hesitated, reasoning that he needed to get as far away from the train as possible.

But then he heard the voice of unreason itself. It was Kirby screeching, "I said, get that money. Danny, you get that money or there'll be hell to pay."

Danny smacked his packhorse on the rump to send it

chasing Bobby's pack animal, and then dug his spurs into his stallion's sides as he raced toward Bobby's idle mount. As he did so, he pulled his pistol from its holster and tried to lay down covering shots to ward off the sharpshooter in the train, knowing all the while that he was too far away to do any good.

Danny reached the startled horse and grabbed the bridle in his left hand as he quickly turned his own snorting steed. He returned the pistol to the holster and rode all-out toward the waiting gang members who were now cheering him on.

He smiled and stifled a nervous laugh, thinking, by God, I'm gonna make it.

A low cracking sound caught up to him and he instinctively hunkered down in the saddle to make himself a smaller target. He braced himself for the inevitable pain of the bullet, but, Danny realized too late, that he wasn't the sharpshooter's intended mark.

His horse crumpled under him, and he felt like he was floating in the hot desert air. Time slowed and his ears quit working, as if someone had clamped their palms over the sides of his head. But then, the old rules of living took control, and he fell like a rock. There was no panic in his descent, no flailing of arms or impassioned curses.

He just fell.

Danny knew that he had stopped falling when he felt a wallop on the back of his head and a pinch in his neck, followed by a headache as big as any canyon. A wave of nausea swept over him and he felt like he would puke. He tried to open his eyes only to quickly shut them against the blinding sunlight. Danny fought to make sense of his situation. He was dazed and flat on his back.

His ears rang and buzzed, yet he could still hear the high-pitched cries and frantic breathing of his horse. His horse, where was his horse? Have to get on my horse and get out of here, he thought.

He tried to sit up.

He pushed up with his arms, and his torso bent at the waist until he was sitting. So far, so good, he thought. He tried opening his eyes again, but that made his head spin before he could open them all the way.

"Stand up you fool. Stand up and get on your horse," he muttered.

Danny tried to stand, but his legs wouldn't budge no matter how hard he willed it. His horse neighed, and he reached out to feel his legs, but found a hot fleshy boulder covered in slick sweat and hair.

"Jesus, I'm pinned down by my horse," he said aloud.

Danny tried pushing the battered horse off of his legs, but it wouldn't move. He opened his eyes and could make out the outline of his horse. He heard galloping coming his way.

"Hold on, Danny," he heard Walt shout.

He could make out Walt's silhouette as he rode toward him.

Danny heard another rifle shot and saw dirt kick up in front of Walt and his mount. Walt let loose a torrent of curses and turned around and headed back to a safer distance.

The hoofbeats of Walt's horse grew distant.

Soon, Danny heard the combined retreat of the whole gang. Only smart thing to do, he thought. They wouldn't be able to get closer than a quarter mile away before they were all picked off one by one by the sharpshooter. There was no cover, and a full-on charge would be suicide.

His head throbbed, so he lay back down on his back and closed his eyes.

There would be no rescue today.

★★★

Danny had lost consciousness. He wondered how long he'd been out. He peered through squinted eyes and noticed that the sun was not overhead. His face was sunburned. His horse's breathing was ragged and raspy. The stallion no longer cried. The end would soon be at hand.

Danny heard footsteps approaching from the direction of the train—the sound of boots walking in sandy soil.

The steps got closer. Danny couldn't bring himself to look at the walker trudging toward him in the Sonoran Desert heat.

He reached down and groped for his pistol, but it wasn't in its holster.

The footsteps stopped, and a cool shade slid over Danny's face.

"Lookin' for this?" asked a steady voice.

Danny opened his eyes to see a middle-aged man dressed like a peddler of pots and pans looking down on him. The man smiled and tipped his hat.

The stranger had Danny's gun in one hand and the muslin bag filled with the passengers' belongings in the other hand.

The man squatted down, and Danny squinted to get a better look at him. The man pulled a handkerchief from a pocket and wiped his brow.

"Well, I'll be damned," said Danny. "Captain Wheeler—alive and well and in the flesh. You should be dead, by all rights."

"Should be, but I ain't," said Wheeler. "Seems Kirby has a powerful need to take that which ain't rightly his, and you have a powerful need to tag along with your big brother no matter what stupid idea pops into his head."

Danny frowned and replied, "They say blood is thicker than water, Captain. Besides, Kirby's done all right by me so far. I ain't got no complaints."

The man smiled and said, "Danny, my boy, that brother of yours will be the death of you."

He cocked Danny's pistol, pointed it downward, and pulled the trigger.

The passenger car swayed back and forth accompanied by the metronome clamor of the rails beneath. Sunlight streamed through the open windows as the passengers dozed. The morning's robbery had tired them all.

Henry Wheeler laid the newspaper across his lap and pulled his recently retrieved pocket watch from his jacket. He flipped open the cover and glanced at it. Considering the little dustup in the desert and the time it took to repair the track and push the destroyed mail car from the line, they were making pretty good time. Another hour until Tucson, he thought. It was supper time and Wheeler was hungry.

He polished his reading glasses and resumed reading the newspaper. Peering over the top of the paper, Wheeler spied the cowboy sitting quietly in his seat smoking a cigarette. He warily watched Captain Wheeler—no longer a Bible salesman, but now a killer.

Several rows of seats behind and in front of Wheeler were empty.

Wheeler wondered if it was him that the passengers avoided or the young outlaw's body that lay in the aisle next to his seat. He had placed a bandana over the dead boy's face—a kindness to Bobby more so than to the passengers. He truly regretted having to shoot the boy, but it couldn't be helped. The railroad would have thought him negligent had he let part of the money, which was within his power to retrieve, get away. He also knew that at least some of the bandits would attempt to recover the lost money making them a target too. Besides, the young outlaw had his watch and wallet.

Bobby had gotten in over his head and had paid the price.

The Fat Man deserved no such courtesy. Wheeler had put him face down on an empty seat, placing the dead man's hat and valise on top of his body.

The engineer had insisted that all of the bodies ride in the freight car, but a stern glance and a firm no from Wheeler had convinced him otherwise. The dead conductor and four guards would ride in the freight car—out of sight and out of mind—but the outlaw's body, and that of The Fat Man, would stay next to him. Bobby, in his present state, was worth an extra one hundred dollars to Wheeler. He aimed to collect the reward as soon as the train pulled into Tucson and didn't plan on bickering with the sheriff, the undertaker, or the railroad over possession of the bodies.

"Water," said a ragged voice.

Wheeler lowered his paper and peered over the seatback.

He raised the paper and continued reading.

"Please," said the voice.

Henry Wheeler set down the paper and uncapped the canteen beside him. He stood in the aisle and pulled Danny up to a sitting position.

Danny's hands were cuffed behind him, and his hair and clothing were caked in sweat and sand.

"Stand up," said Wheeler.

Danny struggled to stand up, and managed in the end.

"Good, your legs ain't broken," said Wheeler. "Looks like you can walk into the jailhouse of your own accord."

"Now sit back down," he commanded as he forcefully pushed Danny back into the seat by his shoulder.

The outlaw groaned. "Feels like I got at least one broken rib and my head hurts somethin' awful."

Danny looked Wheeler in the eyes and cracked a little smile. "Suppose I shouldn't complain. Lucky to be alive. I thought you was goin' to bring me in dead, same as Bobby. After you shot my horse, I thought I'd be next. By the way, you didn't have to put me to sleep with the back end of my pistol."

"Worth more alive," Wheeler said. "Besides, people love a good hangin.'"

"How about that water, Captain?"

"Raise your head and open your mouth."

Danny did as he was told, looking, for all the world, like a starving chick waiting for a worm.

Wheeler grudgingly poured water from the canteen into Danny's mouth. He poured until Danny sputtered and started to choke.

"More," said Danny.

"That's enough."

"Just a little more, Captain. I won't be no trouble."

"No more water. No pee breaks until we get to Tucson."

6

News of the robbery spread quickly.

The cowboy made for the nearest saloon and parlayed his eyewitness account into enough free drinks to put him in a drunken stupor. Hunched over a table, he snored peacefully until the bartender had him thrown into the street, where he picked himself up and staggered into an alleyway to continue his napping.

The older couple made their way to the mercantile, where they purchased a bottle of *Doctor Koenig's Nervine* to settle their ragged nerves. Between the two of them, they consumed half the bottle on the spot while they recounted the calamitous tale to the proprietor and all assembled customers before crossing the street to the hotel. There, they rented a room, ate a hot supper, and retold the story a second time to the waitress. Stomachs full and brains idling, they ascended to their room where they lay down on the bed and promptly fell asleep.

The young mother and her children were met at the train station by her husband. Upon seeing their father, the children bounced in place shouting, "Papa, Papa, the train was robbed by outlaws. There was lots of shooting and a Bible salesman killed one robber and captured another."

The poor woman burst into tears. The confused husband tried, to no avail, to quiet the children and console his weeping wife.

He piled his family into their wagon. The children continued to bounce and yammer.

"Quiet down right this minute, or you'll be gettin' the switch," he said.

"What the hell happened?" he asked his wife.

"It was horrible."

"What was horrible?"

"Papa, you missed all the fun," shouted the boy.

"I said to pipe down. Can't you see your momma's in a frightful state?"

"Papa, Papa…"

"Here, suck on this," said the man impatiently. He produced two pieces of stick candy. The children grabbed the candy and began to gnaw on it—teeth be damned.

"Now Judith, tell me what happened on that train."

"I don't want to talk about it, John. It's too painful. If you really cared about me, you would see that I'm all flustered and in need of some comforting. But no, it's always about you."

She turned away from him and said, "I just want to go home."

He urged on the horses and mumbled under his breath, "Jesus and Mary, guess I'll have to read about it in the papers."

"Papa, Papa, more candy."

After the passenger car emptied, Wheeler waited alone guarding over Danny and the bodies of Bobby and The Fat Man.

The engineer entered the car and walked back to Wheeler's seat.

"I want to thank you for how you handled that back

there," said the engineer.

"Thank you for not giving away my presence on the train," replied Wheeler.

The engineer shook his head. "It's a pity about the conductor and those guards," he said.

"The man had no nerve. Had he remained on the train, he most surely would have given me away. Still, I'm sorry that he died," said Wheeler.

The sound of approaching footsteps ended their conversation. A porter entered the car and made his way toward them.

"Sir, I was told you got some luggage you need help with."

"Get up," Wheeler said to Danny. "It's time to go."

The engineer nodded at the bodies in the aisle. "Help me carry them out to the luggage cart, son."

The porter grabbed Bobby by the ankles while the engineer lifted under his arms. They lugged him to the door, returning soon for The Fat Man. Lifting to no avail, they were reduced to rolling him to the platform, then heaving his body over the railing onto the luggage cart.

Wheeler carried his bag in one hand and his rifle in the other and prodded Danny forward.

"Stay with those saddle bags, and make sure the bank signs for the proper amount of money that was recovered," Wheeler said to the engineer.

Wheeler set his bag on top of the bodies. The porter pushed the cart from the train station toward the Pima County jail and the sheriff's office. Danny trudged behind the cart and Wheeler followed him with the rifle.

The people of Tucson watched the parade.

Most stared in silence, some clapped, and a few whistled.

∗∗∗

The porter propped the bodies against a street-facing wall of the Pima County jail. Wheeler tipped the porter, and he departed for the train station as a crowd gathered to gawk at Bobby and The Fat Man.

"How'd you two like to make some money?" Wheeler asked two boys in the crowd.

"You bet, mister," said the older of the two.

Wheeler tossed a coin to each of them, and to the younger boy, he said, "Go get the undertaker and tell him he's got a couple of customers at the jail."

To the older boy, he said, "You keep an eye on these bodies and make sure nobody molests them or tries to carry them off."

"Yes sir," said the older boy. "You can rely on us."

Wheeler urged Danny up the steps of the sheriff's office. The sign above the door read, *Sheriff Robert H. Paul, Tucson.*

They entered the office. A wiry, weather-beaten man sporting a red handlebar mustache propped his feet on an old scarred desk at the back of the room. Long red hair cascaded from beneath a stained brown ten-gallon hat and a star was pinned to his chest that read Deputy Sheriff. Half a dozen rifles stood at attention in a rack on the wall behind him.

He paused from cleaning his fingernails with a penknife and raised his blue eyes to take in the two men standing in front of him.

"What can I do for you gentlemen?"

"I need to talk to Sheriff Paul," said Wheeler. "Got one for the jailer and two for the undertaker."

"Sheriff ain't here. Up in Prescott on county business."

"When will he be back?"

"Ain't due back for at least a week. I can relieve you of your prisoner. What's he done?"

"He's one of five men who robbed the train and made off with a shipment bound for the banks here and El Paso. One of the dead men is a gang member, and the other is a confederate of the gang, keepin' lookout on the train. They murdered five railroad men too, so there's that."

"How much was in the safe?" asked Smith.

"Ain't for me to say," said Wheeler.

"Reckon upwards of eighty-thousand," Danny helpfully volunteered.

Wheeler nudged Danny between the shoulder blades with the barrel of his rifle.

The deputy whistled, tipping his hat back on his head.

"They get away with all of it?" he asked.

"Most, but I got back a little. The bankers are taking custody of it back at the train. That'll be my next stop. The bank, and then the telegraph office," said Wheeler.

"And who would you be, Deputy?"

The deputy looked Wheeler up and down before answering.

"Deputy Sheriff Aldous Smith," he said slowly. "And who are you?"

Wheeler reached into his jacket pocket and pulled out a folded piece of paper. He shook it open and handed it to Smith.

"Henry Wheeler from the Pinkerton Agency. I'm under contract with the Southern Pacific Railroad."

He pulled out his wallet and opened it, revealing his silver Pinkerton badge.

Aldous Smith stood up behind his desk and rested a

hand on the butt of one of his holstered pistols.

"Pinkerton and the Southern Pacific got no sway in Pima County," Aldous said.

Wheeler nodded at the paper, still unread, in Smith's hand.

"As you can see, I'm also on special assignment from the U.S. Treasury to use any and all authority and force necessary to discharge my duties for the government of the United States."

Aldous gave Wheeler a crooked smile.

"We ain't a state," he said.

"You're a territory, and the federal government's police powers still take precedence in a territory, Deputy Smith. Besides, I believe Arizona Territory would one day like to be the state of Arizona. The governor of Arizona Territory might not take too kindly to a deputy sheriff impeding the investigation of an agent of the federal government who has the power to influence the process toward statehood."

Aldous stared at Wheeler, the smile gone.

Danny watched the exchange with amusement.

"Best not challenge his authority. The Captain don't like that," Danny said.

Wheeler said nothing, and Danny continued, "So, Captain, you're a damn Pinkerton man now. Hell, that's the same as fightin' for the Yankees. I thought you had more honor than that."

"Well, Deputy, you got room for this one? Best I be on my way," said Wheeler.

"I think we got an empty cell," said Aldous.

He returned the paper to Wheeler and made his way through a door adjacent to his desk.

Danny and Wheeler followed Aldous Smith into a small

room where a grizzled old man lay sleeping on a cot.

Deputy Smith roused the man by the shoulder until he woke.

"Toby, wake up. You got a new prisoner."

The little man stood slowly and scratched the stubble on his cheek. He reeked of sweat, coffee, and whiskey.

The jailer rubbed his rheumy eyes and blinked at Danny.

"I'll put him in cell three next to Jasper and Abe. They can keep him company, as they like to talk."

"No, this one's important. I want him in the back by himself. No communicatin' with the other prisoners," said Aldous.

"All right then. Cell eight's a good ways off from the other prisoners," said Toby. "Let's go, son."

Toby took charge of his prisoner, and Aldous Smith and Wheeler followed the jailer to make sure that Danny was secured in the cell.

"You goin' after them other men?" asked Deputy Smith.

"Yep, and the property of the U.S. government."

"Can't give you no posse. All available men are helpin' the cavalry at Fort Lowell track down an Apache raiding party. You can raise a posse of your own, but it'll cost you."

"No need," said Wheeler. "I can do it all myself."

Danny entered the cell, and Wheeler removed the handcuffs. Toby closed the cell and locked the door.

"I'll need a receipt for the prisoner and the deceased men," said Wheeler to Aldous. "The railroad will pay for the undertaker. Just a pine box on boot hill will do."

"No," said Danny. "Don't bury Bobby on boot hill. He was a good kid even though he put in his lot with us. His family is named Bristow, and they live south of Limon.

They ain't got much money, but they can come get his body and bury him on their land."

"Can you find his folks?" asked Wheeler.

"I believe we can," said Aldous Smith.

"All right then, turn him over to his family. The railroad will pay for the embalming and the coffin. Not the fat one though. He gets the pine box on boot hill."

"Thanks, Captain," said Danny.

"I'm sorry things had to end this way, Danny. You would have been better off to go out on your own and keep clear of Kirby."

"Kirby's my brother," said Danny. "Where he goes, I go."

Wheeler said nothing and turned to leave.

"Wait up, Captain Wheeler."

Wheeler turned to face Danny.

"I just want to say that I didn't kill any of those men. Things just got out of hand and went all helter-skelter."

"I didn't reckon you did," said Wheeler. "But you'll hang just the same for keepin' the wrong company."

"Except in the war, I ain't killed nobody. See, it's important to me that you know that, even if it don't make no difference in how things end," said Danny.

7

Wheeler's meeting with the banker was short. After inspecting the retrieved money and the engineer's voucher, he obtained a receipt. He then guaranteed the banker that the U.S. Treasury would make good on the remainder of the transfer from the San Francisco mint. He went to the telegraph office and sent identical messages to Charles J. Folger, the Secretary of the Treasury, Allan Pinkerton at the Chicago office of the Pinkerton Agency and the San Francisco office of the Southern Pacific Railroad.

It read:

Special Agent Henry Wheeler
Aug 23, 1882

Agent Wheeler intervened in robbery. Identity of robbery suspects confirmed as Barksdale gang.

Danny Barksdale captured, 2 dead, 3 still at large, 5 RR employees killed by suspects. All passengers unharmed.

Partial recovery of U.S. government property now in possession of First National Bank, Tucson.

Prisoner remanded to Pima County Sheriff's office.

Will pursue suspects and property with all due haste.

Predict successful conclusion of case.

Wheeler paid for the telegrams and inquired about the location of the livery. He would purchase a horse in the morning and board it on the train. He and the mount would travel, courtesy of the Southern Pacific, back to the location of the holdup, and he would track the gang from there.

Wheeler remembered what Danny had said about not killing any of the men. He believed Danny and wished that things had turned out differently. He hoped for a quick hanging and that it would be as painless as possible. Danny deserved to be punished, but he didn't deserve to die.

Yet, someone had killed those five railroad men. He had removed the two least dangerous outlaws from the equation. Those who remained must be the most desperate and dangerous of the bandits. He knew Kirby, but knew nothing of the other two men.

Yet, knowing Kirby was enough.

8

Wheeler bought a bottle of whiskey and had the hotel kitchen make him a sandwich. He carried the meal up to his room.

The dusty chamber had a bed and a wooden chair. An empty basin sat on top of a small table. No pictures or decorations adorned the small room.

Wheeler crossed the musty room and opened the window to get a breeze. There was a soft knock on the door, and he opened it to find a young girl holding a pitcher of water.

"Fresh water for the basin, sir. Chamber pot is under the bed. The outhouse is behind the hotel."

He took the pitcher from her and marveled that she was strong enough to carry it up the stairs.

"Will you be needin' anything else, sir?"

"No, thank you," he said.

Without a word, she skipped to the stairs and scurried down them, happy to be done with the chore of seeing to the lodger in the upstairs room.

He closed the door.

Wheeler poured water into the basin and scooped the liquid up with his cupped hands to rinse the dirt and sweat from his face and neck. The cool water refreshed him. He looked for a towel, and finding none, he stood in front of the window until the dampness evaporated from his skin.

The hour was getting late now, and the room began to cool off. He sat on the bed and ate his sandwich and drank his rye from the bottle as he stared at the patterns on the cracked wallpaper.

It had been a long day. The whiskey was going to his head and making him drowsy. He lay down on the bed, his head sinking into the pillow. Wheeler glanced at the door one last time. He closed his eyes and fell asleep.

Henry Wheeler's sleep was fitful and filled with uninvited dreaming.

***

Black railroad tracks, laid down over an old farm road, snaked through half-melted snowy woods. A hardwood forest, bereft of leaves, leaned in toward the tracks from both sides. This stretch of rails wandered through five miles of wooded land before opening up on a section of fields and pastures to the west. The woods provided a break from the bitter wind of northern Virginia in early February.

Captain Wheeler and his five men had wandered four hundred and fifty miles in less than a month—almost always by night, mostly on foot, but sometimes on stolen horses, or in the wagons of friendly farmers or Confederate spies. To help escape detection, none wore uniforms.

The miles had taken their toll on the ragged squad of Rebel commandos. Threadbare, ill-fed, and constantly dodging Union patrols, they made their way from one secret contact and cache to the next, always searching for an opportunity to lessen the enemy advantage in supplies and material.

The bloody Battle of Nashville in December '64 had decimated the Army of Tennessee, and the Confederates were now in a desperate situation. Because of the devastating loss, General Hood, disgraced, had resigned his commission in January. But not before he had secretly tasked Captain Wheeler to command a renegade band charged with raiding Union supply lines, and, whenever possible, repurposing those supplies to the Confederate cause.

And, so, the raiders fought on.

At first, Wheeler could do little to inflict any real damage on the Yankees. He and his men had to content themselves with the occasional burning of a barn full of conscripted crops and smoked meats destined for the Union troops. Truth be told, Wheeler wondered if he was striking a blow against the occupying army, or simply depriving his own starving countrymen. Nevertheless, he reasoned, an empty Union belly might even the odds of a fair fight between Yankees and Rebs.

It was a one-legged Rebel telegraph clerk who first gave Wheeler the idea to rob trains. His men were starving and this Confederate veteran had heard rumors that there were some Rebel soldiers who needed feeding.

The clerk sought out the commandos by wagon and lugged along some smoked ham and hardtack to fatten their bellies. For his efforts, he had nearly had his throat slit, but he eventually convinced Wheeler that he was, indeed, a friend.

He told Wheeler about a Yankee supply shipment coming by train. He said that the Union had taken over all of the telegraphs and lines in this part of Virginia and that he and his fellow telegraph operators were privy to the movements of those trains.

Before the fellow slipped back to town, he had outlined the itinerary of the supply train and had given Wheeler the names and towns of other telegraph operators whom he thought would be sympathetic to the cause.

The clerk's tip had been a godsend. For some reason, supply trains were lightly guarded, and the crews on the trains rarely put up a fight. A single train might be loaded to the brim with ammunition, woolen blankets, boots and food. Usually it was easier to destroy the supplies with fire, thus denying their use by the enemy, but sometimes Wheeler had the use of wagons, and they were able to have spies smuggle the goods back to the Rebel lines.

The effectiveness of Wheeler's tactics was evident by the fact that he and his men had a bounty on their heads. Today's robbery was the seventh so far, and his men were getting very good at this line of work.

The cawing of crows perched in the treetops interrupted Wheeler's thoughts. His men had been instructed to maintain silence. Private Kirby Barksdale knelt beside Wheeler, half buried in dead leaves, his grim countenance staring down the tracks. He watched big Sergeant Morris bent over a track, his rear in the air and an ear to the cold steel. He had been in that pose for almost an hour. Now, he jumped up from the track and came running into the tree line, shouting, "Train's comin', Captain."

Wheeler told Private Barksdale to pass the word that the train carrying the Yankee supplies would be entering the zone of operations soon. He gave the order for the two men farther down the track to give the final axe blows to the trees on either side of the tracks. Wheeler watched as they came crashing down, making passage impossible.

His men hunkered down in the leaves and the litter

under the trees. They breathed into the leaves so that the fog from their breath would not give away the ambush. The men could hear the approach of the train now, and their muscles tensed in anticipation of a fight. The sound got louder, and now they could feel the power and mass of the iron horse. The smokestack on the engine billowed gray-black soot and smoke. The cowcatcher formed an ever-larger spearhead as it traveled low to the tracks, leading the way toward the waiting band of men.

The engineer, seeing the trees in front of him, applied the brakes, and the train began a labored stop.

The train passed the spot where Danny Barksdale, brother of Kirby Barksdale, lay in wait. Wheeler saw him jump up from his hiding spot and chop at a large oak tree until it slowly fell across the tracks preventing the train from backing up and escaping the way it had come. The hulking iron beast, trapped in Wheeler's cage, snorted steam and smoke, yet could not move.

Wheeler's men stormed the engine. A young lieutenant urged two green privates to fire upon the Confederates. Kirby knelt in the tree line, took aim, and fired at the lieutenant who fell to the floor of the engine. The two privates—boys no older than sixteen—threw down their weapons and raised their hands. The engineer and the stoker—evidently Rebel sympathizers—pushed the young lads from the engine to the ground.

Wheeler approached the engine, and the lieutenant stood up nursing a wounded right arm. The stoker kicked the lieutenant's pistol across the floor of the engine. It skittered out the door and onto the ground.

Captain Wheeler picked up the lieutenant's weapon from the gravel and dirt. The Union officer jumped to the ground and faced Wheeler.

Wheeler said, "I give you my word as an officer of the Confederate States of America that no harm shall come to you and your men and that your surrender shall be an honorable one. At this late stage of the war we wish you no ill will. We only seek the destruction and confiscation of supplies and material that may damage the prospects of the Confederate war effort. You have my word, Lieutenant."

The lieutenant looked Wheeler in the eyes and slowly removed his battle sword from its scabbard and presented it to the Confederate captain.

"Lieutenant Rice," he said.

"And I'm Captain Wheeler, sir. I must now insist that you remove yourself and your men to the rear of the train so that we might keep an eye on you. I ask you not to interfere with our task."

The Yankees marched to the caboose followed by the engineer, the stoker and Wheeler and his men. Danny Barksdale was waiting there, his rifle trained on three young privates who sat on the ground with their hands on their heads.

"Howdy Captain Wheeler. These boys here are all that's in the caboose. They tell me that there's a couple of soldiers in each of them two freight cars."

Wheeler faced the Yankee officer and said, "Lieutenant, it would go much easier on your men if you were to convince them to surrender. We are sworn to commandeer this train and we will not hesitate to use force."

The young lieutenant made his way to the first freight car and banged on the door with his fist.

"Porter, Simmons, get out here. We are surrendered and are prisoners of Captain Wheeler."

The door slid open and the two stunned privates blinked at the daylight, their hands raised in the air. The lieutenant repeated his entreaty at the next car and two more young men joined the ranks of the captured.

Captain Wheeler accompanied the Yanks to the caboose where they joined their comrades. Danny watched as the new arrivals sat with the other men—ten Union soldiers in all. He stepped back and leveled his rifle at Lieutenant Rice thinking that a threat to the head of the snake would control the body.

"Private Johnson," said Wheeler, "I need you to relieve Danny and continue guarding the prisoners."

Private Arlo Johnson, who resembled a scarecrow more than a soldier, took Danny's rifle.

"Best you keep it trained on the lieutenant," said Danny to Arlo.

Captain Wheeler clapped Danny on the shoulder and said, "Fine job, Corporal. I need you and Private Wainwright to fetch the wagon and the horses. It's high time we finish up and get on our way."

"Yes sir," replied Danny, who hustled the other soldier down an old dirt road that ran perpendicular to the railroad tracks.

"All right," said Wheeler. "Let's see what we got."

★★★

Sergeant Morris climbed into the first freight car and inventoried the shipment.

Wheeler shouted to Morris, "Well, Sergeant, what fine goods are the Yankees gifting to the Southern cause today?"

"Looks to be mostly blankets, beans, and ham hocks, Captain."

"Winter will be comin' to an end soon, so we'll burn the blankets and take the beans and meat," said Wheeler.

As if on cue, Danny and Wainwright appeared beside the freight car with the wagon and horses.

"Pull that wagon beside this car and let's throw down the ham hocks. Kirby, you and Sergeant Morris go see what's in the other freight car," said the Captain.

Morris jumped from the car to the wagon and then to the ground. He and Kirby disappeared into the second freight car as the others began loading up the wagon with the ham and beans. The Yankees looked on from their positions by the caboose under the watchful eyes of Private Johnson.

"That's enough," said Captain Wheeler to the loading crew. "Let's see how much room we need to leave for the contents of the other freight car."

Wheeler turned and addressed the open door of the forward car. "Sergeant Morris, what's in that car?"

Silence.

"Sergeant Morris, Private Barksdale, I need your report. How much room do we need to leave in this wagon for the contents of that freight car?"

Again—no reply.

The other men stood stock still, barely breathing, so as not to make any noise.

"Damn it, Morris, we aint' got all day."

Muffled conversation could barely be heard from the second freight car. It sounded like Sergeant Morris and Private Barksdale were engaged in a heated debate.

Wheeler pulled his pistol from his holster and took several steps toward the now silent freight car.

"Tarnation, Sergeant, just what the hell are you doin'? I need an answer now—not later."

Sergeant Morris poked his head out of the door of the freight car and Captain Wheeler stopped short in his tracks.

"Sorry, sir. Just more ham hocks, beans, and blankets."

Morris hesitated and then blurted out, "And a big old safe, Captain. It's mighty heavy."

Wheeler paused and said, "Kirby, I need you to come with me."

Kirby jumped to the ground and followed Wheeler to the seated prisoners.

"Lieutenant Rice," said Wheeler, "I need to know what's in that safe."

"I'm not at liberty to divulge that information, Captain."

"Kirby draw your pistol," said Wheeler in an icy voice.

"I'm prepared to die if need be," said Rice.

"No need to give up your life, Lieutenant, though I don't doubt that you would."

Wheeler walked over to the soldier who appeared to be the youngest.

"Private Barksdale, put the barrel of your pistol up to the temple of this boy's head."

The engineer and the stoker who had been eating their lunches paused in mid-bite. Private Johnson tensed his grip on his rifle. Kirby, unsure of the order, drew his gun and stared at his Captain.

"You heard me Private, do as you're ordered."

Kirby Barksdale grinned at Lieutenant Rice and put the gun barrel against the frightened youngster's head. The boy looked at Rice who was, in turn, intently watching Wheeler.

"I'm going to count to three and then, if you don't tell me what's in that safe, I'm going to tell Kirby here to pull the trigger. Do you understand me Lieutenant?"

Rice did not answer.

"One…"

Kirby cocked his pistol.

"Two…"

"Greenbacks," said Rice.

"How much?" said Wheeler.

"I truly don't know."

Wheeler glared at the lieutenant.

"But, it's a lot. That's all I know. I swear it on the lives of my men."

"Can you open it?"

Rice sat stony faced and glared back at Wheeler.

"I asked you a question, Lieutenant. Can you open that safe?"

"Yes, Captain Wheeler, I can open the safe."

"Well, then, get up," said Wheeler. "Kirby, accompany the Lieutenant to the safe. Private, carry on your guard duty."

Lieutenant Rice made his way to the freight car. Sergeant Morris reached down and pulled the lieutenant up into the car. Captain Wheeler climbed into the car behind the Yankee officer.

"All right, sir, open the safe, or Private Barksdale will return to carry out my previous order," said Wheeler.

Rice crouched down next to the safe and turned the combination.

Right-click, left-click, right-click, left-click, right-click.

He turned the handle and pulled the safe door open revealing neatly stacked bundles of Union currency.

Morris whistled, and said, "Enough money there for all of us to live off of for a long while, Captain."

"Enough for six men, or maybe enough to help turn this war around. Let's load it up in the wagon and get it back to our lines," said Wheeler.

Captain Wheeler and Lieutenant Rice jumped down from the car and started the journey back to the caboose and the waiting prisoners.

"Thank you, Lieutenant. I'm sorry that I had to threaten you and your men that way. I assure you that under less dire circumstances I would never have acted as I felt compelled to act earlier. You have my apologies."

Rice walked beside Wheeler and said, "I took you for a gentleman, Captain, but it appears…"

The Union officer gasped and then sucked in a big gulp of air as he grabbed for his back and clawed behind himself. Rice's legs crumpled and Wheeler instinctively held the Lieutenant under his arms.

Wheeler slowly lowered Rice to the ground. The handle of a large hunting knife protruded from Rice's back, the blade buried deep within his body.

Captain Wheeler let go of the inert body and slowly stood. His hands were covered in Rice's blood. He wiped them on his pants and stared in disbelief at Kirby Barksdale.

"March on back to them Yankees, Captain," said Kirby as he leveled his rifle at Wheeler.

Sergeant Morris jumped from the freight car and pointed his rifle at Captain Wheeler too.

"Sarge, what's goin' on?" asked Jimmy Wainwright.

"Don't you worry son, everything's going to be all right. Just help us get this Union money and we'll all be rich," said Sergeant Morris.

"But, what about the Captain?" said Jimmy. "This ain't right, Sarge."

"Danny, get a rifle and come on up here and help me," said Kirby.

"Kirby, are you crazy? We get caught and we'll face a firing squad. You killed that Yankee lieutenant in cold blood," Danny said.

"Then I guess we best not get caught, little brother," said Kirby.

The Union prisoners began to stand up.

"You just stay where you are and nobody will be any the worse for wear," said Kirby.

"Now Arlo, you keep your gun on them Yankees. Don't let them stand up," Kirby said to Private Johnson, who did as he was told.

Kirby poked Captain Wheeler in the back with the barrel of his rifle.

"Get on now, Captain."

"Kirby, you're cheating our army out of vital cash that could help us win the war or sue for better terms in an armistice."

"This war's all but over, Captain. You're just too stubborn to admit it. The only cause worth fightin' for now is the Barksdale cause, and the Sergeant Morris cause," Kirby looked at the two young soldiers, smiling, and continued, "...and the Privates Wainwright and Johnson cause."

Wheeler stopped at the circle of prisoners.

"Now sit," said Kirby as he poked Wheeler in the back with his gun.

Wheeler did as he was told and Kirby continued, "But there ain't goin' to be no Captain Wheeler cause. You're too damned honorable to think of yourself. Ain't that right, Captain?"

Wheeler said nothing.

"You two," said Kirby pointing at the engineer and the stoker. "Get over here and sit."

"But we're loyal Virginians. We ain't got no truck with these Yankees," protested the engineer.

"Just get over here and sit," Kirby replied.

Two more men were added to the clustered bunch of prisoners. The twelve dejected men eyed the five rifles aimed at them.

"Let's look for somethin' to tie them with," said Danny.

"Ain't goin' to be no tyin'," said Kirby who spun and shot Private Johnson.

Sergeant Morris shot Wainwright, and both privates dropped to the ground.

"What're you doin'?" shouted Danny. "No, Kirby, this ain't right."

Kirby and Morris shot the seated men as fast as they could. They picked up the murdered privates' rifles and used them too. In the midst of the chaos and carnage, they reloaded the Springfields and emptied them into the crowd of prisoners. The men tried to stand, but could not rise fast enough to rush their executioners. Kirby and Morris finished the job up close with pistols. Wheeler saw bodies slump all around him until he, too, was felled. He felt a searing pain in his chest and left shoulder. Peripherally, he saw the engineer try to stand. He made it to his knees, only to be cut down by Kirby. The engineer, a heavy man, fell on top of Wheeler pressing his head into the melting snow.

Wheeler tasted mud and blood.

★★★

Henry Wheeler was accustomed to nightmares. He had lived with them for almost two decades. The robbery on the train and the run-in with Kirby and Danny had triggered tonight's little sideshow. Granted, most nights were not quite so intense or so real.

The heat of a summer night in Tucson only added to his discomfort. He sat up in his darkened hotel room and willed his eyes to cut through the pitch black, but they could only just make out the void of the open window.

He stood and crossed the room sensing his way to the window by the barely perceptible breeze. Wheeler unbuttoned his shirt. He quickly removed it, and wadding it into a ball, tossed it in the general direction of his luggage. He ran a finger across the old hardened scars on his shoulder and chest.

After all these years the closed holes still burned. He reached behind him and traced the exit wound on his back—the entrance wound's twin. The flop sweat was evaporating now. He breathed deep the dry, hot air, but felt no relief from the heat.

He absent-mindedly picked at the scar tissue on his chest. No exit wound here—only a one of a kind trauma—pieces of the bullet still lodged in his chest. Sometimes he swore he could feel hard metal lumps leaping about in time to the beating of his heart.

Yet, of all his wounds, he thought, the one that would never heal was the psychological trauma of betrayal.

Wheeler stuck his head out the window and looked both ways. The end of the street where his hotel was located was dark and quiet. No one about, everyone safely tucked into bed.

The other direction, however, was livelier. He squinted his eyes at the gaslights that illuminated the saloons.

He could just make out the shapes of people walking about in the night at the far end of the street. He listened to the laughing, singing, and cursing that mingled with the sounds of music that floated up to his window. At the far end of the street there was no sleeping and no nightmares.

Wheeler walked back to the bed and lay down. He reached beside the bed for the whisky bottle that he was sure had fallen onto the floor.

No more dreaming, he thought, as he raised the bottle to his lips.

Allan Pinkerton scanned Wheeler's telegram.

Reading between the lines, he guessed that despite his detective's bland description, the robbery had been a bloody mess. Knowing Wheeler as he did, he had no doubt that he would pursue Kirby Barksdale to the ends of the earth if that was what it took to bring him to justice.

The thing about Henry was that no matter his personal feelings toward Barksdale, he would always do the honorable thing. That was the trait that he most admired in Henry. Captain Wheeler might want to kill Kirby on the spot, but he would do everything within his power to bring the bandits in alive so that they could be tried, found guilty, and hanged.

And hanged they would be.

He could have sent a much younger man, a much more ruthless man to hunt down the Barksdale gang, but the other trait that he admired in Henry was his prudence and attention to his adversaries' character—what the new science of the mind called the criminal psyche. It was ironic that it had been Kirby himself and his betrayal of Henry that made him such an eager student of criminal behavior and perversion.

He scratched the chin hidden beneath his beard and dislodged a bit of his morning breakfast of dried oatmeal—a ritual meal in honor of the austere early days in his native Scotland. It tumbled to his stomach and came to rest with the other odd crumbs of food, dandruff, and dry skin.

Pinkerton opened the folder on his desk titled Personal/Confidential – Special Detective Wheeler, Henry. He removed the photographs and spread them out on his desk. The first and oldest photo was taken of Henry as a prisoner in the Old Capitol Prison in Washington D.C., just prior to the end of the war. The South had not yet surrendered and Henry had been charged as a Confederate spy and accused of taking part in the murder of fourteen men—Union, Confederate, and civilian—in order to steal the money contained in the safe being transported aboard a Union cargo train. Henry stared into the camera with an intensity that belied the precarious state of his health and the parlous nature of his existence.

As the former head of the Union Intelligence Service, Pinkerton had heard tell of the exploits of the Confederate guerillas led by Captain Wheeler. He had personally dispatched his own undercover spies into the Southern countryside to ascertain the Rebels' whereabouts so as to stop their plundering.

Certainly, he had wished to put an end to their activities, but he had also admired the audacity and skill with which they had undertaken each of their robberies. Pinkerton had brought train robbers to justice before the war, but he had never before dealt with an adversary like Henry. Short of attaching a platoon of men to each transport—men that the Union could scarcely afford to spare—Pinkerton had seen no sure-fire way to stop Wheeler and his men.

Well, when he had discovered that the leader of this band of commandos was imprisoned in the capitol, he had known right away that he must interview him, if for no other reason than to learn the tricks of the train robbery trade from one of its earliest and most accomplished practitioners. After all, he had reasoned, the future of the United States would rely on the expansion of the railroads. More railroads would mean more railroad thievery; and Pinkerton's future would rely on protecting railroads from the criminals who would follow them like flies to molasses.

From the day that he had met Henry—barely hanging onto life, gravely wounded and unfairly maligned as a thief and murderer—he had marveled at his honor, devotion to duty, and his tenacity to live.

Pinkerton quickly learned that the charge of murder was simply preposterous. The military tribunal had determined that the Rebel commandos had seized the train and executed the prisoners who had bravely fought off their attackers. Wheeler and the two Confederate privates, they argued, had simply been casualties of the fighting. However, any detective worth his salt could have put holes through the prosecution's logic.

For starters, the investigators had simply been lazy. All of the bullets used in the slaughter had come from Confederate weapons. It would have been highly unlikely that the Union soldiers would have defended themselves by shooting Wheeler and the two privates with Confederate arms. Furthermore, Henry had been found underneath a number of bodies indicating that he had been part of the group of imprisoned men. The two Confederate privates had been shot outside the ring of the executed, probably surprised by their comrades who had murdered them.

Pinkerton had worked on prying the truth from Henry. The breakthrough had come when he had disparaged the honor of Henry's charges, Private Wainwright and Private Johnson. He had accused them of being a party to murder. Henry had leapt to their defense and in a torrent of words confirmed Pinkerton's hypothesis.

Over the course of the next week, Pinkerton and Henry developed a level of trust and admiration for each other. They talked of the war and honor and duty. Pinkerton told Henry of his fervent abolitionist beliefs and Henry told Pinkerton about his duty to his fellow Southerners and his way of life and that while neither he nor his family were slave owners, he could no sooner desert the South than he could desert a brother in need.

Both men had known that the war would end soon, and Henry had conceded to Pinkerton that if the Confederacy surrendered, then as an officer, he would be honor-bound by that surrender. When the inevitable surrender came, Henry said, he could live happily without slavery, and he would start life anew.

But, Henry had no chance of living.

It was then that Pinkerton decided to find a way to save Henry's life.

Pinkerton had first proposed that Henry resign his commission in the Confederacy and then join the Union Army. He promised Henry that he would not be required to fight his fellow Confederate soldiers and that he would instead be sent west to fight Indians. He had told Henry that he believed that if he personally laid out the particulars of Henry's situation to President Lincoln, then the charge of spying would be dropped and his death sentence would be commuted.

Henry, however, categorically refused to join the so-called "Galvanized Yankees" even if doing so would have saved his life. Again, he chose death before dishonor.

So, Pinkerton had changed tack and personally asked Lincoln if he could find the time to meet with an extraordinary person who had become a dear friend, despite having fought for the Confederacy. As a favor to Pinkerton, Lincoln had agreed to grant Henry one hour of his time. And so, on Saturday afternoon April first, 1865, Henry and the commander in chief of the United States had the first of several chats.

Abe and Henry had gotten along so well, that three hours later, the president's secretary had to insist that Lincoln end the visit to attend to pressing matters of state. That same evening, suffering from a bout of insomnia, Lincoln had Henry brought from his prison cell under cover of darkness to his quarters, where the two men had talked into the early hours of the morning. Lincoln and Henry had continued to meet several more times, and soon the Confederate Captain and the war-weary president had become friends.

Later, Lincoln had confided to Pinkerton that Henry had become like a son and had given him hope that once the war ended, the nation could be healed.

It was upon hearing of Lincoln's affectionate feelings toward Henry, that Pinkerton had made his new proposal. Could the president, he had asked, see his way to pardoning Henry under the condition that Henry be remanded into Pinkerton's care? Furthermore, Pinkerton continued, he would personally see to Henry's training as a detective.

Pinkerton had pressed his case that Henry may have been a spy, yet he had acted honorably and with care to operate as a soldier rather than a scoundrel. Surely, a pardon for someone like Henry would illustrate the spirit of reconciliation that the president so hoped for.

On April ninth, 1865, one day before he was to be hanged, the president pardoned Henry. That same day, General Robert E. Lee surrendered his Army of Northern Virginia, thus precipitating the end of the war. Six days later, on April fifteenth, 1865, Lincoln was dead from an assassin's bullet.

President Lincoln's death had been a hard blow for Henry. He had become a devoted friend of the president, and the manner of his death hit close to home. The parallel between the treachery of assassin, John Wilkes Booth, and his own would-be executioner, Kirby Barksdale, was not lost on the former Confederate.

The government had asked Pinkerton to aid in the investigation of the assassination and the prior conspiracy, and Henry had insisted that he, a Southerner, be allowed to restore some semblance of honor to the South by participating in the mission. Pinkerton, fearing that Henry had not sufficiently healed, had reluctantly agreed.

Henry was still too weak to pursue the assassin who had fled to Virginia by way of Maryland. However, a Southerner himself, he had been able to gather evidence and reconstruct the plot against the president without arousing suspicion. He had quickly identified the conspirators who were rounded up and later hanged or imprisoned.

Henry would later curse Booth for his treachery and his foolishness. The melodramatic actor's cowardice had done nothing to reverse the South's inevitable loss. Had Lincoln lived, he had reasoned, the burden of Reconstruction would have been less harsh.

Henry had insisted that his involvement in unraveling the conspiracy and bringing the conspirators to justice remain unknown and thus, the pivotal role that the Confederate captain had played in history was largely unrecognized.

✶✶✶

Henry's capacity to learn the detective trade was unparalleled. He had learned everything that Pinkerton could pass on to him, and he quickly became one of the agency's best detectives. He had always treated Henry like a son, well, not really a son, but a younger brother, and the two men trusted each other implicitly. Henry respected Pinkerton and, of course, owed him a debt that could never fully be repaid. For his part, Pinkerton took delight and pride in the younger man's development.

In no time, Henry was taking on the agency's most important cases. He proved himself time after time. He possessed all of the characteristics that Pinkerton deemed important in a detective. He was intelligent yet instinctual, brave yet cautious, unyielding yet judicious, and above all, honorable and honest to a fault.

Since suffering a stroke, Pinkerton had been forced to reduce his responsibilities in the agency. His sons, William and Robert had taken over many of the leadership duties but were jealous and combative toward each other. Henry had proven a calming influence upon the two young men. He feared for the future of the agency without Henry.

And although Pinkerton loved him as a son, he knew that Henry was not entirely without weakness. Being the detective and spymaster that he was, Pinkerton had undertaken a thorough investigation of Henry, as he did all of his agents.

Pinkerton had discovered that Henry wrestled with demons.

He was obsessed with making Morris and the Barksdale

brothers pay for their war crimes. Henry devoted considerable time, effort, and agency resources into tracking down the three men. In the summer of 1876, Henry had learned that Sergeant Morris had died of yellow fever in a Louisiana bayou. Now, he was beyond earthly justice.

Henry sank into a deep depression and was troubled by nightmares. Pinkerton's agents reported that he sometimes drank too much. It never interfered with his work, but Pinkerton had witnessed firsthand the destructive nature of alcohol on his friend, Ulysses S. Grant, and considered drink to be a vice that was best avoided entirely.

Henry continued to excel in his work and was instrumental in many delicate cases. He was also personally responsible for saving the life of Pinkerton's son William after he had been captured during a botched investigation. The debt, it seemed, had been paid.

Finally, in 1880, the Pinkerton Agency had been hired by the Department of the Treasury and the Southern Pacific Railroad to protect shipments of U.S. currency and coins from the San Francisco Mint. There had been a rash of unsolved robberies, and Henry had led the investigation. Gradually, he had come to suspect the involvement of the Barksdale brothers. This knowledge, of course, only stoked Henry's desire to personally be the agent to bring the case to a conclusion.

He had cultivated an informant who worked as a clerk in the Mint. With Henry's guidance, the informant had arranged a meeting with a disgraced former Confederate major. The informant had purposefully fed the major the details of a large shipment from the Mint to banks in Tucson and El Paso.

Pinkerton had reluctantly given Henry permission to be

the agent designated to accompany the shipment and to bring in the gang. He hoped that Henry would be able to conquer his demons if he brought them in. Unbeknownst to Henry, he had hedged his bets by assigning another agent to ride along hidden in an empty freight car.

Henry's telegram alarmed Pinkerton. The loss of the money and the deaths of the railroad employees and the agent greatly complicated things. The secretary of the treasury was furious with the agency, and the Southern Pacific threatened legal action if the money was not recovered.

Pinkerton removed the other two photos from Henry's file. The first was of a young man who looked to have the world by the tail—in the prime of life, glad to be alive, the carnage of the war behind him, and a brilliant future ahead of him. The second was a recent photo of an older man weighed down by an overwhelming obsession and too much drink.

For Henry's sake, he hoped that the successful conclusion of this case would calm the demons in his soul. For the sake of Pinkerton and the agency, he hoped it would be the redemption that ensured a successful transition from father to sons.

10

Aldous Smith whistled a happy tune as he sat cleaning his fingernails. He tried to count up the recent stagecoach and train robberies that had occurred within, a more or less, two hundred and fifty-mile radius.

He made a notch on the wooden desktop for each one. He counted nearly two dozen total robberies in the last year. He subtracted the ones that had been solved or that involved just one or two outlaws. What was left was a half-dozen train robberies with dynamited safes. None had been solved, and no money had been recovered. Each time the railroad had decided not to make a big fuss about it.

He tried to figure up how much money might be missing, but stopped when it got difficult to add so many numbers. All he knew for sure was that it was more money than a man could spend in a lifetime.

The next thought that popped into his head was that he was only making twenty dollars a month plus whatever the sheriff decided to give him as a share of arrests, serving papers, and whatnot. The sheriff made good money, but Aldous would never be sheriff. You had to win an election to be sheriff and no one with any pull owed Aldous enough to help him win.

Of course, Maggie at the saloon made him some extra money. But that hardly counted.

That Henry Wheeler was an odd one, he thought. Old man like that couldn't possibly be a threat to anyone, much less a whole gang of outlaws—even goin' so far as to say he wouldn't need a posse or no help to go after that gang.

"Hmm, don't figure. Must be more to the man than meets the eye," he said to himself.

Sure was tight-lipped about what happened on that train and what he was after. Aldous never trusted a man that kept to himself too much—it just wasn't friendly.

"Pshaw, I can bring 'em in all by my lonesome. Don't need no posse," Aldous said, mocking Wheeler.

That Danny Barksdale wasn't any better, Aldous thought. Why, he hadn't said as much as boo, since they locked him up. Even after Aldous had laid it all before him, about how on account that the railroad had so much sway in the territory, and the heinous nature of the crime (five men dead, no less), and how the circuit judge was partial to a good hangin', even after all that, he still didn't have nothin' to say. Most men, they know they're goin' to die, they want to spill their guts. Only natural. But Barksdale, he just shrugs and says, no foolin' Deputy?

"Yep, only one way to figure it...," said Aldous to himself.

"Danny Barksdale don't think he's stayin' in jail."

11

The big table by the back was reserved for high stakes poker. It took a special kind of card player to sit at *the table*. For starters, the price of admission to this altar of gambling was that the house got ten percent of each player's ante. No I.O.U.s, no promises, no friendly wagers. Strictly professional, and you best not sit down unless you could afford to lose.

The table was made of solid maple and had intricately carved mythical beasts and bare-breasted maidens cavorting around its circumference. It was large and heavy and had come all the way from Chicago by wagon, years before the railroad had made it to Tucson. Two men had died transporting it, one drowned crossing a river and another shot through with Apache arrows.

The saloon employed an old man, whose only job was to polish the table and empty the spittoons that sat next to each of its ten chairs. It sparkled and shined, even by gaslight. And, unlike the rest of the saloon, it even smelled good too, on account of the beeswax polish.

Tonight, six men and the saloon's dealer hunkered down to do battle at the table.

Maggie watched the game from the other side of the bar. Three locals and three out-of-towners, plus old bald Joe the house dealer sat around the table. The out-of-towners all appeared to be run-of-the mill cowboys—hardly high rollers, thought Maggie. They had ridden in late and trail weary.

Joe sat at attention, ready to dispense cards.

Mike Dawson, who owned southeastern Arizona's biggest mining operation, chewed on a toothpick. He scratched his ear and raised twenty dollars. The banker, A.W. Burnett, a short, stocky man with a full head of gray hair and an even fuller belly studied his cards, made a sour face and folded. He threw down his hand in disgust.

Maggie didn't know the man who sat next to him. He was a wiry cowboy with a crooked smile and quick eyes. He nursed an injured arm in a sling. He signaled with his good arm for another drink.

"I'm out," he said cheerfully. He began drumming his fingers on the top of the table until another out-of-towner, a big man with thin lips and three days of stubble, gave him a dirty look.

"Sorry, Kirby," said the bored man.

Kirby shot him a second dirty look and he shut up. He sat on his hands to keep them still.

"I thought you said your name was Roy," said the banker.

"Roy's my middle name. Some folks who've known me a long time still call me by my first name," replied Kirby.

The third local, Archie Mann, owned the mercantile. He had a perpetually haggard look due to his wife and nine daughters who rode roughshod over him morning, noon and night. Maggie was surprised that he was even allowed out of the house.

Archie knocked three times on the tabletop and Joe skimmed three new cards his way. He added the cards to his hand and fanned them out, studying them. He arranged them, moving them about to achieve the best hand.

"Anytime," said the third cowboy who had an x-shaped scar on his forehead.

Archie quietly said, "Well, I guess I'm out too." He lowered his cards face down to the table and smiled sheepishly at the dealer.

Joe showed no emotion.

The cowboy with the scar rapped twice on the table and Joe shot two cards to him. He picked up his cards and threw twenty dollars into the pot. Maggie searched for a tell in his mannerisms, or a tic on his deep-creased face, or any other sign as to the hand he might hold. The x-shaped scar on his forehead made him look like a penitent on Ash Wednesday. She thought he had the greenest eyes she had ever seen.

He looked across the room and met her gaze.

Maggie looked away and the cowboy's eyes returned to his cards.

A new girl named Jenny brought the injured cowboy his drink. She picked up his empty glass and he stealthily patted her on the bottom. She turned her hip and pulled away from him, shooting him a sour look.

Jenny moved over to the man called Kirby and put her hand on his shoulder.

"Ain't interested," he said.

She angrily crossed back to the bar and sat down next to Maggie.

"You give up easy," said Maggie.

Jenny looked up at her and replied, "Them cowboys got plenty of money, but all they care about is cards. I don't understand men. Beats me how three mangy cowboys got so much money."

Maggie looked at the pot in the middle of the poker

table trying to guess how much it totaled.

"What's wrong with the cowboy with the gimpy arm?" Maggie asked.

"You see him smile? He ain't hardly got any teeth and he stinks."

"So, give him a bath and don't let him kiss you," Maggie said.

She blew a kiss to Jenny as she walked over to the big table.

Maggie pulled up a chair and put her hand on the wiry cowboy's left thigh.

"Well, hello darlin'," he said, smiling.

"Well, hello to you," she said.

She rubbed his thigh and played with his greasy hair.

"Don't look like your heart's in the game," she observed.

"Maybe you got somethin' else in mind?" he said.

"Got a room, top of the stairs."

Maggie nodded to the staircase.

"Good idea," Kirby quickly interjected. He looked over his cards at his partner.

"How much is this gonna cost me?" said the cowboy to Maggie.

"Don't matter. My treat," said Kirby. "Knock yourself out." He threw some money on the table in front of Maggie who quickly scooped it up.

"Thanks, Kirby. I mean Roy," said the injured cowboy.

Maggie took the cowboy by the hand, and they stood and walked to the staircase.

"What's your name, cowboy?"

"Levi," he said. He put his hat on and quickly moved his good hand to Maggie's bottom.

Maggie pushed his hand away and said sternly, "You

gotta wait, Levi. Show some restraint."

"I'll try my best. It's been a while, ma'am."

"I wouldn't of known," she said. They continued to the stairs.

"Speakin' of a while, how long's it been since you last bathed?" Maggie continued.

"Case you ain't noticed," said Levi, "nothin' but desert and scrub all around. Water's kinda hard to come by."

"How about we get started with a nice warm bath. It'll relax you."

"That cost extra?" said Levi.

"Your friend got you the deluxe package. A bath is just the first course, cowboy."

"Yeah, but bathin' takes time. I don't know if I can muster up *that* much restraint."

"Won't take no time at all," said Maggie. "Besides, your friends are gonna be playin' cards all night. You don't want to get bored again, do ya?"

They arrived at the top of the stairs. An older woman exited a room with a wad of bed sheets under her arm.

"Hey, Sal, bring up some towels and hot water, will ya? Oh, and a bottle of rye."

★★★

Maggie poured another drink for Levi. He hunkered down in the warm bathwater, only his head sticking up. He smiled dreamily and sighed.

"Phtttt." Levi made a noise with his pursed lips.

"Say, Maggie, this bath sure does hit the spot. You were right, I am relaxed."

His speech was noticeably slurred.

"What happened to your arm?"

"This?" Levi flapped his hurt arm still in the sling,

splashing water out of the tub.

"That ain't nothin'. Fell off my horse."

He submerged the arm, sling and all, under the bath water and resumed his impersonation of a turtle poking its head out of its shell.

Maggie sat behind Levi, reached around his head and brought the glass up to his lips.

Levi slurped the rye from the glass and swallowed.

Maggie lathered up Levi's face with shave soap.

"Now for a nice shave, cowboy."

She opened the straight razor that lay on the small table next to the tub.

She stroked the razor up the side of his face.

"You do that real good, Maggie," said Levi.

"So, Levi, what are you and your friends in town for?"

"Business," said Levi matter-of-factly, sounding as if he had rehearsed his answer.

"What kind of business, honey? Kirby your boss?"

"In a manner of speakin', I suppose he is."

"Who's your other partner—the hard-lookin' one?"

"You mean Walt?" asked Levi. "He ain't so hard. Just lookin' out for our interests, that's all."

Maggie lifted Levi's chin and shaved the whiskers on his neck.

"Ya'll don't seem like businessmen. You ain't peddlers or merchants. Kinda rough in the saddle," she said.

Levi thought a second before he answered.

"Nope, just cattlemen," he said.

"Most cattle come in by rail now. Surely, you ain't drivin' herd?" she said.

Maggie offered Levi another drink and he slurped and smacked until the glass was empty.

"Nah, we come to town to negotiate a deal for cattle to ship in later."

Levi paused and said, "And we're meetin' a friend."

"Who's this friend of ya'll's?"

"Well, he's my friend, but he's Kirby's brother."

Maggie smiled and continued shaving Levi.

"He ain't anything like Kirby, is he?"

"Heck no," said Levi. "Kirby ain't easy goin' like his brother."

"You say he's a friendly feller, huh?"

"Oh yeah, me and Danny, we been through thick and thin. Ain't nothin' gonna come between us. Why I'd do anything for him and he'd do the same for me."

"You know Levi, you say that ya'll are businessmen, but you don't look like you got much money. I was thinkin' maybe you'd like to come back tomorrow night for another deluxe package, but I don't think you can afford it."

Levi sat up in the tub, and taking umbrage at Maggie's remark, said, "You don't know nothin', Maggie. My share's more than you can count, I guarantee. I got enough for a lifetime of deluxe packages."

Maggie finished the shave and returned the razor to the table.

"You got your money in some bank somewhere?"

"Bank, heck no. We don't trust no banks. Them bankers is pick pockets. Why, they'll rob a man blind."

She pinched Levi's cheek and said, "You sure ain't car-ryin' it on ya, Levi, cause I seen you naked as the day you was born, and I can't for the life of me figure where else you could hide it."

Levi laughed and splashed the water with his good hand.

"Maggie, you sure are somethin'. Of course we ain't carryin' it on us on account that would be stupid and 'sides there's way too much money to lug around. Why it'd take a big old wagon to fit all that money in. We got us a place about a day and a half ride from here that only we know about."

Maggie spoke carefully.

"You mean you and Kirby and Walt?"

"And Danny," added Levi. "We been workin' real hard and was doin' pretty good too. Wasn't till just recent that our work really paid off though. We ain't gonna need to work no more."

"Well then, I stand corrected. I guess I'll be seein' you again tomorrow night, huh Levi?"

"No ma'am, we ain't gonna be in town after tonight."

"You finishin' up your business tonight, Levi?"

"You bet," he said. "Gettin' Danny and leavin' tonight."

Levi felt his face and said, "All clean and slick as a whistle. Am I cleaned up enough?"

"Tell you what," said Maggie as she stood behind the tub.

She unfolded the towel and held it out between her outstretched arms.

"Stand up Levi, and let me dry you off."

Levi stood unsteadily, and Maggie wrapped the towel around him. She began to towel him off until he was reasonably dry.

"I need to go down to the privy real quick. Why don't you lie down on that bed and make yourself comfortable? I'll be back as soon as I can," Maggie said.

Levi fell backwards onto the bed.

"Aw, c'mon Maggie. Can't ya use the chamber pot? I'm

startin' to get sleepy. Besides, Kirby and Walt will be finishin' up their card game soon, and I gotta be ready to ride."

"A gal don't like to do that in front of a man, Levi. Just a few minutes are all I need."

"Hurry up, Maggie. I showed enough restraint for ten men."

"Just take me a bit, you won't even know I been gone," she said as she slipped out the door.

✶✶✶

Maggie hugged the wall of the upstairs hallway, making sure that Levi's partners below couldn't see her leaving the room. She made her way to the last room and slipped inside. It was a storage room for linens, foodstuffs, and alcohol. She crossed to a small desk and put a pad of paper and a pencil under the garter beneath her dress. She peered out the window to get a glimpse of the alley behind the saloon.

All clear, she thought. The outhouse was a short distance away.

She opened a door at the back of the storeroom and descended the stairs to the alley. Maggie glanced both ways and scurried to the outhouse. A black cat padded across the alley and disappeared into the darkness. Somewhere, a couple of dogs barked a conversation.

Maggie slipped into the privy and shut the door behind her. Taking out the pencil and pad of paper from her garter she printed a short note, tore it from the pad and hid it in the bodice of her dress. She returned the pad and pencil to the hiding place.

She took a deep breath and composed herself. If she was going to get caught, this is where it would happen, she thought.

In one swift movement, she opened the door and ran down the alley, not daring to look back.

She arrived at a small tarpaper shack. Opening the door, she went inside and stood waiting to catch her breath. Against the far wall, on a cot, lay a sleeping boy.

Maggie knelt at the cot and gently roused her six-year-old son.

"Harry, Harry, wake up baby. It's Mama."

The boy, who was facing the wall, slowly rolled over to face her.

Maggie smiled at her son and brushed the tangle of red hair from his forehead and eyes. Freckles covered his face. Even in the dim light of the moonless night, his pale skin glowed.

My little angel, thought Maggie.

"Hello, Mama," Harry said in a slight voice. He smiled at his mother, and raising up, he wrapped his arms round her neck and hugged his thin body to hers.

Maggie kissed the boy's cheek and softly said, "Honey, I need you to do something for me."

"What, Mama?"

She removed the folded note from her bodice and holding it out to her son, said, "Harry, this is a very important note. I need you to run over to the sheriff's office without anyone seeing you and I need you to give this note to Uncle Aldous."

Maggie held Harry by the shoulders and looked straight into the little boy's trusting blue eyes.

"Do you think you can do that for me?"

"Sure, Mama. I can get over to the sheriff's office quick as lightening. Just watch me, I can run fast now that I'm six."

"I'm sorry, Harry, but I can't stay to watch. I have to get back to the saloon."

Maggie paused and looked very serious to make sure that Harry understood what she was about to say next was important.

"Now, listen up Harry. I'm going to leave, and when I shut the door I need you to count to one hundred before you go to see Uncle Aldous. OK?"

Harry nodded his head and took the note from his mother.

"That's a good boy. I love you, and I'll see you in the morning."

Maggie stood and walked to the door. She opened it a crack and peered down the alley. Once she was sure that all was clear, she stepped outside and said quickly to Harry, "Remember, don't let anybody see you."

Maggie stood silently outside the shack until she heard Harry's small voice.

"One…two…three."

She hiked up her dress and ran.

✦✦✦

Levi lay asleep on the bed.

Maggie shook him awake.

He rubbed his face and yawned.

"Damn, Maggie. How long you been gone?"

"No time at all, Levi."

"What time is it?" he asked.

"About two in the mornin'. Don't you worry. Kirby and Walt are still sittin' at the poker table."

Maggie undressed and stood at the foot of the bed.

Levi lay on his back watching her. He whistled and said, "Oowee! You are a fine-lookin' woman, sure enough."

Maggie laughed and said, "Levi, I believe that you would call any woman that walked through that door, 'fine-lookin.'"

Maggie leaned over Levi and ran her hand through his shampooed hair.

"You know, Levi, I ain't partial to Tucson. There ain't nothin' here for me and you got so much money…"

She climbed into bed and lay down beside him.

"I was just thinkin', maybe I could be persuaded to settle down. I ain't got nobody and you ain't got nobody. Maybe you could be my man and I could be your woman. You could take care of me and I could take care of you."

Maggie propped herself on an elbow and looked into Levi's eyes.

"I need a strong man to take care of me. Would you like to take care of me, honey?"

Maggie ran her index finger down Levi's chest.

"You won't regret it," she said.

12

"Ninety-eight, ninety-nine, one hundred."

Harry jumped out of bed and grabbed his overalls. He slipped them on over his bedclothes.

His mother had asked him to take a note to Uncle Aldous and to make sure that no one saw him. She had said that it was important.

During all of Harry's few years on earth his mother had never asked him to do anything important. She had always taken care of him, and now it was his turn to take care of her.

He wadded the note up in his small fist and ran out the door. His heart pounded in his chest as he sprinted to the sheriff's office.

Harry exited the alley and stopped to scan the main street for anyone who might be wandering about.

No one.

Run, run, run, he thought to himself. Don't stop, don't stop.

His mop of red hair bounced up and down on his head.

Step, bounce, step, bounce.

Harry passed the dry goods store and the lumberyard.

Getting closer, he thought.

Barber shop and then the diner.

At last, the sheriff's office.

He bounded up the two steps to the porch, turned the door handle, and barged in.

"Uncle Aldous!"

Aldous Smith, startled from his sleep, bolted up from his chair and drew his pistol on Harry.

"Damn, boy," he said. "Don't ever do that again. I nearly put a bullet through your skinny hide."

Harry stood stock-still and stared at the pistol in Aldous's hand.

"What are you doin' out by yourself? It's late, boy. Where is your Mama?"

"I got an important note from her to you," said Harry.

Aldous holstered his pistol and held out his hand for the note.

"Well, give it here, boy. Ain't got all night."

Harry hesitantly walked over to the big sheriff's desk and Aldous's outstretched hand.

He didn't understand why his Mama had anything to do with Uncle Aldous. He was a mean man. He had beaten Harry more than once. Mama, too.

Harry remembered the last time. Aldous had been drinking, and he came into their room unannounced. He'd told Mama that he wanted all of her money, but she didn't want to give all of it to him on account of they needed some to buy food.

Aldous didn't listen to Mama. He just laughed and walked over to the place where she hid her saloon money. Mama had tried to stop him, but Aldous hit her hard in the back of the head knocking her to the ground.

Harry sat with her for what seemed like forever before she woke up. He was afraid that Aldous had killed Mama.

Harry gave Aldous the note.

Aldous unfolded it and slowly read the note, his lips moving. Harry tried to make out what he was saying, but

Aldous noticed him watching and turned his head to the side.

When he finished, Aldous said, "You done good, boy. You run on home. I can take care of this now."

Harry turned to leave, and Aldous said, "Boy, don't forget, don't let anyone see you, and don't tell anyone about this. You hear?"

"Yes, sir," said Harry as he shot out the door.

✶✶✶

Aldous read the note again:

Train robbers in the saloon.

Kirby and Walt playing poker.

Levi upstairs in my room. Getting him good and drunk.

Danny is Kirby's brother. They have come to bust him out.

Levi says a treasure is hid about a day's ride from here.

Trying to find out more.

— Maggie

Aldous folded the note and stuck it in his pocket. Aldous's hunch had been right all along. It all added up, he thought. Danny seemed so cock sure of himself. He didn't seem to be worried about hangin' because he didn't think it would happen.

So, Danny's brother had come to break him out of jail. Well, that could be a bloody affair, Aldous thought. Likely, the gang would just as soon get the job done under cover of darkness and leave without a ruckus—no one the wiser. That would be preferable to a bunch of shootin' and noise and maybe even dyin'.

It would take surprise for that to happen. Well, there would be no element of surprise now. But the gang wouldn't know that.

He could send for a couple of men to help him and lay an ambush for them. They'd never know what hit 'em.

Aldous thought about the possible reward on the gang. Wheeler had said that the railroad and the U.S. government took a special interest in this case. Maybe there'd be a little more than usual in it.

Of course, he might get himself killed, and then no amount of reward would do him any good. There was risk involved in any decision that a man made. The smart thing was to minimize the risk and maximize the reward. That's how bankers and businessmen made their money.

Aldous preferred getting paid without any bullets.

'Course the reward wasn't the only money available. The treasure that the gang had hid would be a heap bigger than any reward. If he could get his hands on that, well, he'd never want for anything again.

Minimize the risk and maximize the reward. That was how the smart folks did it. The gang wanted Danny out of prison without any risk, and Aldous wanted money without any risk.

Aldous had Danny and the gang had money.

Aldous slapped the desktop.

No need for fightin', he thought. We'll make a deal.

Walt kicked Kirby's leg under the table.

He glanced at Walt who furtively nodded at the door. Kirby watched the deputy walk to the bar and order a drink.

The lawman turned to scan the room, his back leaning against the bar. He lifted the drink to his mouth and wedged the rim of the glass under his red handlebar mustache. Kirby tried to gauge the man's intent.

Tall, lean, two well-used pistols in a quick-draw rig rested low on the man's hips. He pushed his ten-gallon hat back on his head. A red mane of hair hung to his shoulders. Clean clothes and even cleaner fingernails—this was a man who didn't like to get his hands dirty.

Kirby's gaze lingered a bit too long, and the two men's eyes met. Kirby looked away, but the deputy continued watching the game.

He wondered how many lawmen were guarding Danny. He figured that the sheriff would be home asleep—unless the deputy had sent for him. That would leave at least a jailer, maybe another deputy. If they were to kill this peacock deputy right here and now, then maybe they could just waltz into the jail and free his little brother.

What the hell was takin' Levi so long, he thought?

He knew that he could count on Walt in a fight, but if they started shooting now, then Levi would be on his own.

If he had a third man that he could count on, then that

would seal the deal. They could take out the deputy and free Danny.

"Cards, sir?" said the dealer.

Kirby looked at his hand and said, "No cards, I'm good."

The game continued as Kirby kept an eye on the deputy who slowly sipped his beer.

Kirby peeked over his cards and the lawman tipped his hat.

Kirby nodded back and Aldous gave him a friendly smile.

The deputy set his drink on the bar and slowly walked toward the big table.

Walt put a hand under the table and rested it on the handle of his pistol.

"Hold up," whispered Kirby. "Let's hear what he has to say."

The other gamblers didn't notice the situation unfolding before them, but Joe the dealer overheard Kirby's command and prepared to duck. Walt saw the nervous expression on the dealer's face and said, "Stay."

Mike Dawson, whose turn it was, replied, "What do you mean, stay? It ain't your turn friend."

The sound of a bottle breaking followed by a woman's scream pierced the raucous noise of the saloon. A hush settled over the bar.

Aldous stopped dead in his tracks, the smile gone from his face. His eyes gazed up to the rooms at the top of the stairs.

That was Maggie who screamed, he thought.

Kirby and Walt watched the deputy, now distracted.

"You damn Jezebel," a drunken voice shouted from inside the room.

"Levi," said Kirby and Walt, simultaneously.

Two gunshots boomed from the upstairs.

Kirby and Walt drew their guns. Aldous dove under a

table, and everyone scattered. Those close to an exit high-tailed it out, and those in the middle of the saloon scrambled for cover.

The outlaws overturned the big table to give themselves some protection from gunfire.

A splash was heard followed by a heavy thud.

A moment later a small river of sudsy water mixed with bright red blood ran under the door of Maggie's room. It cascaded down the stairs forming a miniature waterfall.

Walt fired his pistol in the general direction of the cowering deputy as he and Kirby ran for the door.

Aldous went after them, his guns still holstered.

"Wait up," he shouted. "We need to talk. I got a proposition to make."

Aldous watched helplessly as Kirby and Walt galloped out of town.

✶✶✶

Aldous reentered the saloon.

The drinkers, gamblers, and saloon girls straightened the overturned tables and chairs.

"Get back to what you were doin' folks. The law will take care of the rest," announced Aldous.

He retrieved his beer, turned his back to the bar, and scowled up at Maggie's closed door. Maggie's sobbing could be heard outside the room.

Aldous finished his drink, banged the empty mug on the bar, and quickly strode to the stairs, his red hair flowing behind him. He stamped up the wet steps careful not to slip in the last rivulets of suds and blood.

He threw open the door, entered, and slammed it behind him.

The tub, empty but for a small pool of bloody water, lay on

its side. Levi's naked body was sprawled across it. His dead eyes stared skyward and his mouth formed a small circle of surprise. Two big bullet holes were neatly arrayed in his chest. On the floor by his open hand lay a straight razor, a thin line of red blood congealing on the sharpened edge of the blade.

At the foot of the bed, Maggie sat in a little ball, a sheet loosely wrapped around her naked body. She hugged her legs up to her chest and buried her head in her crossed arms, crying quietly.

Aldous went to her. He lifted up her chin forcing her to look up at him. A long red cut stretched across her forehead. Blood ran into her eyebrows where it jelled. He crouched next to her and put his face close to hers. She gazed into his eyes and stifled her weeping.

Quietly, so as to keep anyone downstairs from hearing, he asked her, "What'd you go and do Maggie?"

She said, "He tried to kill me, Aldous."

Aldous squeezed her face and repeated his question, "What'd you go and do Maggie?"

Maggie said nothing. She sat on the floor shaking with the fear of almost dying by Levi's hand and the new fear of Aldous's white-hot anger.

"I'll tell you what you done, girl."

Aldous squeezed harder and said, "You done cost me a fortune. You cost me a fortune and a chance at a new life. That's what you done, Maggie."

"But Aldous, he come at me with a razor. You see what he done to me. I shot him in self-defense."

"Well, you must of done *somethin'* to get him riled up enough to want to kill ya. What did you go and do? Huh, Maggie?"

"I'm tellin' you, Aldous, I had him good and drunk and

he was talkin' free not holdin' back, you know—just blabbin'. I was tryin' to find out where they stashed their money. He was answerin' me anything I asked, so I just asked outright where the money was hid. I swear he was about to tell me, and then he gets this look in his eyes and gets real quiet. Next thing I know, he comes at me with that razor, screamin' that I was a Jezebel. So I did what I had to do."

"What you had to do? Don't you see, Maggie, you didn't have to do a dadgum thing."

"But Aldous, I did it for us."

Aldous backhanded Maggie with his free hand, the utterance of the word 'us' angering him beyond control.

"For us? Maggie, I don't know where you got it in your head that there was any such thing as us. There ain't no us—only me."

"But Aldous, with that kind of money, we could make a new life. You, Harry, and me could be a real family. I could be an honest woman for once."

Aldous kicked at Maggie, but missed.

He said, "I had me a surefire plan, and you flat out ruined it."

He paused and then continued, "A once in a lifetime opportunity come to me, and I had a plan to capitalize on it, Maggie. It's good as gone now. I'll never get within a mile of them outlaws."

Maggie's eyes glazed over.

"You been mean to Harry and me, Aldous, but I always thought that deep down inside you really loved us," said Maggie.

Aldous scrunched up his nose as if smelling something nasty, and said, "You been nothin' but trouble to me ever since that San Francisco whorehouse I found you in."

He took a step toward Maggie and said, "I got a mind to kill you right here."

Maggie reached under the sheet still wrapped around her and lifted up Levi's pistol. She held it in both hands pointing it at Aldous.

"You seen my handiwork, Aldous. I'm a good shot with a gun."

Aldous raised his hands to head level.

"Hold on, Maggie. A little slap don't deserve a bullet."

"Now that I know where we stand, I suggest that you go on back to that jail, and stay away from me," said Maggie.

"You committed murder and I aim to put you in the jail to await trial," said Aldous.

"It was self-defense, and if you don't back me up, well, I got plenty to tell about them things that you done before we got to Tucson. There's a lot there for you to worry about. I think you know what I mean."

Aldous kept his hands in the air and backed up to the door.

"Oh, and I ain't givin' you none of my earnings anymore," said Maggie.

Aldous pointed his index finger at Maggie and said, "You best be lookin' over your shoulder, Maggie, 'cause this ain't over by a longshot."

He backed out the door and slammed it shut.

Maggie kept the gun trained on the door until she no longer heard Aldous's boots clumping down the wooden steps.

14

Aldous briefly considered going to Maggie's shack and beating up on Harry to teach Maggie a lesson, but thought better of it when he imagined Maggie walking in on the whoopin' and shooting him dead with Levi's gun.

She was right, she was a good shot, thought Aldous.

Besides, during his walk from the saloon to the office, he'd had time to ponder the situation. Maybe there was a way to get what he wanted after all.

He opened the door to the sheriff's office. The deputy pocketed a pair of handcuffs from the desk and took two rifles down from the wall. He laid them across the desk and added three boxes of bullets to the small arsenal.

Aldous tiptoed to the door that led into the jailer's office. He opened it a crack and peeked into the room. As he expected, Toby lay asleep on his cot. The little room reeked of whisky.

He opened the door just wide enough to slip in and stood over Toby listening to the cadence of the jailer's breathing. He removed one of his pistols, and holding it by the barrel and cylinder he raised it over his head.

Aldous brought the heavy pistol down on the back of Toby's head with a sickening thud. A trickle of blood ran down onto the old man's neck. He rolled Toby over and put his ear up to his mouth.

Good, he thought, still breathing. He wanted to make sure that Toby was out of the way, but he didn't want to kill him.

Aldous took the big ring of iron keys from the nail on the wall and unlocked the door that led into the jail. He shut the door behind him, but didn't lock it. The keys jangled as Aldous walked, so he mashed the ring against his body to quiet them.

The prisoners snored and wheezed in the dark cells. Restless turning and coughing could be heard throughout the jail. The deputy walked as quietly as he could to the very end of the cellblock. At last he stood before Danny's cell.

Danny lay silently on his cot, his back to Aldous.

"What can I do for you, Deputy?" said Danny.

Aldous, thinking that Danny had been asleep, composed himself before saying, "We need to talk."

"You been out rousting some rowdies, have ya? I thought I heard some gunshots."

"That would be your friend Levi," said Aldous.

Danny rolled over and stood up from the cot. He walked to the front of the cell and gripped the iron bars.

"I don't know anyone named Levi," said Danny.

"Don't nobody know Levi no more on account Levi's shot dead."

Danny stared straight ahead showing no emotion.

"You ain't goin' nowhere, Danny. That brother of yours—Kirby and his partner Walt—they skedaddled out of town and they ain't likely to come back."

Danny continued to listen and said nothing.

"The way I see it, you're about as likely as a man can be to see the hangman's noose. Judge will be in town day after tomorrow. I figure it's a sure thing you're found guilty, and then two days later, seein' as how it's a comin'-to-town Saturday—well that's a nice day for picnics and whatnot—I reckon that's the day you'll swing. I'll deputize a dozen men tomorrow. Kirby and Walt won't set foot anywhere near Tucson."

Aldous cleared his throat and continued, "Mind you, I tried to make arrangements for your safe passage. I ain't unreasonable, Danny. I went over to the saloon intendin' to make a deal with your brother. I would've exchanged you for a share of the money. But before Kirby and me could talk, well, let's just say things went sideways, and what's left of your gang rode out of town in a hurry."

Aldous held up the bundle of jail keys.

"But, there's still a way, Danny. We don't need Kirby to make no deal. How 'bout I let you go and you take me to the money. The way I figure, you're down two gang members. Surely, you can give me one of their shares and the three of you still come out one share ahead."

Danny remained silent.

"'Course, I'll need your word you'll convince Kirby and Walt that your freedom's worth a share of the take."

Aldous cleared his throat and said, "What do you say, Danny?"

"You're just gonna let me go and hope that I give you a share?" said Danny.

"Not exactly. I'll expect you to wear these while I accompany you to the money."

Aldous held up the handcuffs in his other hand.

"You do this, and you'll be a hunted man," said Danny.

"I'll take my chances. I wasn't cut out to be a lawman nohow.

"You got yourself a deal," said Danny.

Aldous smiled and said, "Here's to gettin' rich."

The old wound in Wheeler's shoulder burned. It felt like someone was poking him with a stick. He slowly opened his eyes and tried to focus them on the thing that was jabbing him.

He lay on his back, concentrating on the blur in front of him. His vision finally sharpened enough to allow his brain to recognize the little girl who had brought the pitcher of water to his room. She repeatedly poked him in the shoulder with her index finger.

Wheeler looked around the room, saw that it was filled with the bright sunlight of morning and said to the girl, "Stop, please."

He sat up on the side of the bed.

"What time is it?"

"Near six-thirty in the mornin', Mister."

"Why are you in my room?"

"My mama sent me to fetch you. There's some men downstairs to see you."

"What men?"

"One's the mayor and the other's the banker."

Wheeler's ears pricked up when the banker was mentioned.

"You mean the banker from the First National Bank?"

"Yes, sir, that's him. He holds the deed on this hotel. Papa says he's a cheat," she said, matter-of-factly.

Wheeler smiled at the girl.

"Tell the men that I'll be down to talk to them as soon as I get dressed."

"Yes, sir."

She exited the room, closing the door behind her.

Wheeler put on his shirt and cinched his belt. He pulled his boots on and reluctantly put on his jacket—it was already too hot to wear it. He gathered up his belongings and his weapons. He kicked the empty whisky bottle under the bed and slowly made his way down the stairs.

His head throbbed with each step.

Sure enough, the banker whom he had dealt with yesterday was sitting in the small hotel lobby next to a tall, thin man with dark hair. The man's beard hung down to his chest.

"Agent Wheeler, we meet again sir," said the banker.

"I'm Mayor Pinckney R. Tully," said the other man, as he held out his hand.

Wheeler shook both men's hands.

"What can I do for you gentlemen?" he asked.

Before answering, the two men led him to a table in a secluded part of the dining room where a pot of coffee sat.

The banker poured Wheeler a cup. He silently sipped the hot, bitter drink.

"It appears that, while you *slept*, an unfortunate series of events unfolded, Agent Wheeler," said Mayor Tully.

"Most unfortunate," echoed the banker.

"Spit it out, gentlemen. What happened?"

The mayor cleared his throat and said, "Well, as I said before, as you slept, it seems that unbeknownst to us, the Barksdale gang came to town with the intention of freeing Danny Barksdale from prison."

"And they bided their time over at the Tough Nut

Saloon," the banker chimed in. "Playing poker. Cool as a cucumber."

The banker paused to catch his breath.

"Why, I was a party to the very card game that these outlaws participated in. Of course, I had no idea who they were."

"So, what happened?" said Wheeler.

"There was three of them," said Tully. "Two played poker downstairs, Kirby and Walt, we believe. The third man, Levi, was in a room upstairs with one of the saloon girls."

"Did they make a move to get Danny out of prison? Where was Deputy Smith?" asked Wheeler.

"You see, Agent Wheeler, that's the thing. Aldous comes into the saloon and starts to go over to the poker table like he's goin' to talk to these two. Then a couple of gunshots are heard from upstairs. It seems that feller, Levi, come at Maggie—the saloon girl—with a razor, and she grabs his own gun and shoots him dead."

The mayor smoothed out his beard and continued, "Well, after that, all hell breaks loose. People are duckin' for cover and runnin' for the hills."

"I thought I might die," said the banker. "It was simply dreadful."

Tully finished the recounting, "Kirby and Walt hightail it out of town and Aldous goes upstairs to find out what happened to Levi."

"So, the gang's down one more man and the breakout was foiled," said Wheeler.

"You would think," said the Mayor.

"What's that mean?" said Wheeler.

"It seems that around six this mornin' some citizens

heard a terrible ruckus coming from the jail. The prisoners were screamin' and yellin' that Toby, the jailer, hadn't brought no food or water. A couple of men go in to see what all the trouble is, and they find Toby knocked out and his head cracked open," said Tully.

"And, Aldous and Danny are missing," the banker interjected.

"This ain't good, is it?" asked the mayor.

"No, gentlemen, this ain't good," said Wheeler.

This ain't good at all, he thought. He could only imagine what the reaction would be if the Treasury, the railroad, and especially, Mr. Pinkerton were to find out. The situation had worsened considerably. Now he had four men to bring in, a fortune needing to be found, and him without a posse, or even as much as one person that he could trust.

"You gonna telegram for help from the Agency?" asked the banker. "We probably ought to let the Treasury know as soon as we can. Don't you think, Agent Wheeler?"

Wheeler's brain churned for a response.

He most certainly did not want to send a telegram. The best outcome for him would be that he kill or capture all four men and retrieve the stolen money. The worst-case scenario was that he ended up dead trying, in which case, it didn't really matter.

In desperation, he said, "No gentlemen, we are not going to send a telegram. You see, I fear that we may have an informant working at cross-purposes against us. There will be no telegrams and you will not mention this conversation to anyone. Do you understand me?"

The two men looked at each other and back to Wheeler.

"We do," they answered in unison.

It appeared that all four men were heading in the direction of the Santa Catalina Mountains. The two pairs of riders had, more or less, taken the same route out of town.

Wheeler dismounted his horse and eyed the scrub and ground for signs of the riders who came this way before him. He had headed north from Tucson travelling light to make better time—little food, but a good amount of water and enough weapons and ammunition to do the job. The mayor had loaned him a buckskin gelding that was strong and used to rugged travel.

It turned out that Tully was well acquainted with the mountains, having prospected them for many years as a younger man. He had drawn a crude map at the hotel, showing Wheeler where he might reasonably find water, shelter, or helpful trails to speed him on his way.

Tully had warned him that there were thousands of places in the mountains where a man might set an ambush—narrow box canyons, sudden steep ravines, and small caves. He would need to keep his wits about him, or risk being taken by surprise.

He figured that Kirby and Walt had about a four-hour head start on him and that Danny and Aldous were about an hour or so behind them. That was a sizable lead, but not insurmountable.

With any luck, he would wrap things up before anyone realized how cock-eyed things had gotten.

He remounted and followed the trail as best he could until he came to the foothills of the mountains. The ground had become rocky and dotted with spikey saguaro cacti that stood like sentinels in the waning daylight. The scent of creosote and sage filled Wheeler's head. The golden light of sunset made the mountains look like they were on fire. It would be dark soon, and the Sonoran Desert prepared for bed.

The signs were confused now, as he entered the mountains from the south. He thought he could make out four distinct riders, but one set of tracks had changed. One of the horses was limping. A front hoof made a shallower impression and a crooked dragging sweep in the dirt. Maybe a rock lodged between a shoe and hoof had bruised the hoof, or possibly the rocky terrain had caused one of the forelegs to twist.

Wheeler dismounted his horse and led it down the narrow mountain trail. Nearly dark now, he looked at the map before he lost the daylight. This trail appeared to be one of the ancient Indian hunting routes that Tully had drawn on the map. It stretched from the south all the way to the northwest side of the mountains in a diagonal direction. That made sense, thought Wheeler. That would put the hideout closer to the railroad.

Soon, the sunlight disappeared all together, and he had to navigate by moonlight. The four riders continued to follow the same trail for another hour or so, until another path diverged to the east away from the original path. Two of the horses took the new path while the other two proceeded on the first trail.

Wheeler traced the signs on the divergent path until he determined that the lame horse had continued on the original path. He doubled back to the first path and followed the lame horse.

Them splitting up might be a blessing in disguise, he thought. Better to chase the two that he had the best chance of catching, dispatch them, and then go after the remaining two riders. It wouldn't hurt any to even the odds—better two against one than four against one, he reasoned.

Wheeler followed the lame horse in and out of the rocks and canyons on both sides of the trail for several hours, stopping, watching, and listening from time to time to make sure that the other pair of riders hadn't snuck up behind him.

A massive boulder blocked the trail, and a new route went around the fallen stone. Wheeler put on his reading glasses and opened his pocket watch. He positioned it in the moonlight as best he could. It was a little past midnight. He reckoned that daylight would come to the mountains in about five hours or so. It was hard to know how fast the outlaws in front of him were traveling, or if he had gained any ground on them. Best to rest the horse and himself. He would keep going around the bend of the trail to establish a redoubt in case the other riders were following him from behind.

He picked up the horse's lead and started to walk when he heard what he thought was a voice. Wheeler drew his pistol and crouched. He listened again, and this time he was sure that he heard voices.

Covering the horse's head with his jacket, he dropped the lead and crept slowly forward. He pressed himself against the rock and peeked around the corner.

Ahead, the trail continued into a tangle of brush and

scrub that prevented him from seeing anything farther. The voice he now heard was loud and clear and unmistakably Kirby's. The outlaw was plainly annoyed with someone or something as he vented his frustration.

"Either shoot that horse or leave him behind—I don't care which. You're slowing us down," said Kirby.

"I ain't gonna do that, Kirby. He's a good horse and he just needs some work on his shoes, some salve and a couple of days rest. I can take care of it when we get to the mining camp. Even at this pace, we'll be there before daylight."

He recognized the second voice as belonging to the outlaw at the back of the passenger car—the one who had killed the conductor. Must be Walt, thought Wheeler.

"Well, I'm tired of waitin' around," complained Kirby. "We got good beds, water, and grub waitin' for us back at the cabin."

"I ain't keepin' you. Get on up ahead. You got no reason to wait on us. I'll be along shortly."

"All right then, you best get a move on cause I ain't savin' you no ham and beans. What's in the pot is gonna get eat up whether you're there or not."

"I don't want any of your old ham and beans. I can make my own grub."

"All right then."

"Well, all right then. I see how you are."

"Yep, that's the situation," Kirby trailed off.

There was a pause in the conversation, and then Kirby cleared his throat and spit.

"I best be goin'," said Kirby.

"You best. Like I said, don't you worry none about us. We'll be just fine," said Walt, sounding hurt.

Wheeler listened to the two bickering outlaws and con-sidered shooting both of them right then and there, but held back on account of the lost money.

Kirby and his horse left, the sounds of their steps reced-ing into the night.

Walt steadied his horse and continued to sweet talk him.

"We don't need them nohow. Ain't that right, sugar lump? You been a good horse and the only true friend I got. Don't you worry, I ain't leavin' you, and I certainly ain't shootin' you."

Wheeler heard what sounded like a kiss and a pat fol-lowed by Walt saying, "You still got plenty of life left in you. You ain't ready for the boneyard yet. We just need us a little rest is all."

Wheeler heard the sounds of buckles and cinches on leather as Walt untacked his mount. He crept up to the bend in the trail and removed his hat and lay on his belly beneath the scrub and brush. His pistol at the ready, he slowly wriggled forward until he spied Walt and the horse.

Walt removed the saddle and blanket and put them on the ground by the rock wall. He left the bridle and reins on the horse and led it to the widest point on the trail.

"C'mon baby, let's have a little lie down," said Walt as he coaxed the horse onto its side. The paint mustang entirely blocked the path now, and Walt lay down on his back too, his bedroll under his neck, and the back of his head resting against the saddle.

He tilted his hat over his forehead and eyes and folded his arms across his chest.

★★★

Wheeler developed a plan, but he wanted to make sure

that Kirby had put some distance between Walt and him before he executed it. He carefully opened his pocket watch and noted the time. He watched Walt sleep for an hour, and then crept forward from his hiding place.

Wheeler stood over Walt as he snored. He pointed his pistol at his stomach and kicked him in the leg. Startled, Walt tried to stand, but Wheeler pushed him back down with his foot and said, "Keep on your back. Unless you want a bullet in your gut, that is."

Walt looked up at Wheeler and laughed before he said, "Well, I'll be, if it ain't the Bible salesman from the train. So, you're the sharpshooter, huh? I didn't figure you had a steady enough hand or a keen enough eye to do that kind of shootin'. Had that cowboy sittin' in the corner pegged for the shooter. Just goes to show, you never can tell. You got my admiration, pardner. Real slick operation, yes sir."

"I'm gonna need you to get up real slow, Walt. That is your name, ain't it?"

"Yep, sure is. You a lawman?"

"In a manner of speakin'. I'm a Pinkerton man on loan to the U.S. Treasury."

Walt laughed again and said, "Oh, well, makes sense then, don't it?"

"What do you mean?" asked Wheeler.

"That was our mistake, now, wasn't it? If we'd stuck to robbin' regular folks then nobody would of paid us no mind. But, you rob the United States government and then it becomes a federal case, don't it?"

"That wasn't your only mistake, Walt. Killin' that conductor in cold blood for starters—and all of them guards.

"I only killed the conductor. Kirby done the others."

"What about the Major?" asked Wheeler.

"Bobby shot him first, then Kirby finished him off. It was his own fault for bein' stupid," Walt said. "There wasn't no way that Kirby was gonna leave any of that money behind just so The Fat Man could ride out on one of them pack animals."

"All right, enough talkin'," said Wheeler. "I'm gonna need you to slowly unbuckle your holster."

Walt began to get up, but Wheeler kicked him in the leg and said, "Nope. Do it while you're on your back. Unbuckle, and let the belt drop to your sides."

Walt did as he was told, and Wheeler said, "Ok, now stand up real slow, and then put your hands behind your back."

Wheeler clamped a set of handcuffs on Walt and cinched them tight. He poked him in the back with his pistol.

"Now face the rocks and stand there until I tell you to turn around."

Walt did as he was told and Wheeler walked to Walt's horse and urged it to stand up.

"What are you doin' to my horse?"

"Nothin'. Gonna be doin' a little walkin'."

Wheeler checked the time. Almost two in the morning, he noticed.

"How far you reckon the mining camp is from here?" he asked.

"Three hours on foot. Maybe more."

They walked back to Wheeler's horse. Wheeler mounted up and said, "Get walkin' and lead the way."

"You got a name Pinkerton man?" asked Walt.

"Agent Henry Wheeler."

"Well, Agent Henry Wheeler, you ain't gonna take old

Kirby by surprise. Only one way into that camp and the cabin's got a view right down the trail. He can see you comin' a long ways off."

"Don't mean to take him by surprise," said Wheeler.

★★★

Walt had switched trails twice since his capture. The present trail ended in a narrow passage barely wide enough for a horse. A man could stretch out his arms and touch the rock walls on either side with his fingertips. Wheeler had dismounted an hour earlier when the trail began to climb. The trail had just as quickly descended, and now the rock closed in on both sides.

Walt quietly led the way. It appeared he preferred talking to horses rather than people—or maybe it was just the present company he'd been forced to keep.

Wheeler smelled the smoke before he saw the opening in the rocks. The sun had just come up in the sky, but its light had barely penetrated the mountains.

He tapped the outlaw on the shoulder with the barrel of his pistol. "Hold up, Walt."

Wheeler put his saddlebag over his shoulder. He pulled his sniper rifle from its scabbard and holding the pistol in his other hand, said to Walt, "Let's take it nice and easy. Stay in front of me and no sudden moves."

They exited the narrow gap into a wide flat plain scattered with boulders and rocks. About a quarter mile across the plain, a curved pediment of rock rose about a hundred feet into the air. The craggy rocks formed a bowl that encircled the small valley. A sloping fan of fallen rock rested against the other side of the bowl, and next to it sat a small shack made from weathered boards. To keep the wind out, the knotholes and the cracks between the boards had been stuffed with old newspapers and mud. Smoke rose from the cabin's rock chimney. The interior was dark save for the faint light of a single oil lamp next to the lone window.

"Crouch down," Wheeler said to Walt.

Wheeler steered Walt with the pistol barrel stuck in the small of his back. They zigzagged from boulder to boulder low to the ground until they had ventured about a hundred yards into the valley.

He rested his rifle in a notch on a boulder and knelt down. He opened the saddlebag, and taking out a box of bullets, placed them next to the rifle and prepared his sniper's nest.

He opened the breach on the weapon and loaded a bullet. He pulled the lever back as quietly as possible, and then cocked the gun's hammer.

Walt silently watched the Pinkerton agent.

When he had finished his preparation, he reached into the saddlebag again and pulled out a single stick of dynamite.

"Turn around," he said to Walt.

"What are you gonna do with that dynamite?"

"Just turn around," said Wheeler.

Walt did as he was told, and Wheeler stuffed the dynamite down the back of Walt's shirt. The dynamite rested between his shoulder blades and against the base of his neck.

"You can't just blow me up, Wheeler!"

Wheeler tied the dynamite tight to Walt's body with a length of twine and said, "I'm gonna light the fuse on this dynamite. I figure somewhere around a couple of minutes before it goes off. Looks to me like it's about a quarter mile to that shack."

Walt tried to run, but Wheeler yanked on the handcuffs and held him tight. He pushed him facedown into the dirt, putting his knee into the small of his back.

He lit a match and touched it to the fuse. The fuse spit and hissed as it came to life. Tiny sparks bounced off Walt's head and neck. Walt wriggled and cried.

"No, don't do this," he begged.

Wheeler pulled him to a standing position and shoved him forward.

Wheeler glanced at the cabin—still no sound or movement.

"Here's the deal Walt. Your job is to make it to that cabin and convince Kirby to put out the fuse."

Walt was off and running before he could finish the sentence.

Wheeler watched Walt sprint across the valley. He was surprisingly fast for a man running with his hands handcuffed behind his back. The outlaw navigated the obstacle course of strewn rocks and boulders with a vigor that amazed the older man. The fuse danced and glowed against Walt's neck.

Wheeler pointed his pistol into the air and pulled the trigger. The sound of the gunshot echoed across the valley.

The lamp in the shack winked out and all was black.

Walt, in a panic, shouted, "Kirby, it's me, Walt! Don't shoot Kirby. For God's sake, you gotta let me in. You gotta help me, Kirby. I got dynamite strapped to my back. Soon as I get close you put out the fuse.

Kirby appeared for a second in the window, a rifle in his hands. He lifted the gun and took aim, but stopped short of pulling the trigger. He moved to the other side of the window, but still didn't take a shot.

Wheeler tried to get a bead on Kirby, but it quickly became apparent that Walt's zigging and zagging prevented both men from getting a clean shot at the other.

Wheeler made sure that Kirby could see him and, panicky, Kirby squeezed off a shot despite Walt obstructing his view. The bullet whizzed past Walt's head, forcing the outlaw to halt and duck down.

He's using a Winchester '76, thought Wheeler, who relaxed knowing that he was easily out of range of the outlaw's weapon.

"Stay there," yelled Kirby.

"I can't," Walt yelled back. "I got dynamite strapped to me. You gotta put it out."

Walt stood up and soldiered on, running as fast as he could.

Wheeler launched a round from his pistol in Walt's general direction to make sure that he didn't stop again.

Kirby let loose another bullet, this one flying by the opposite side of Walt's head.

"Stop your shootin', you're getting too damn close," cried Walt.

Kirby shot again. Walt moved to the left in response and Wheeler saw an opening. He stroked the front trigger and the Sharps angrily discharged its missile.

Wheeler involuntarily closed his eyes. He opened them in time to see the big bullet fly through the open window where Kirby had been just a split second earlier and detonate into a shower of splintered wood as the shack's back wall exploded.

Somehow, he had missed.

Kirby reappeared in the window.

Wheeler frantically reloaded. He doubted that he would get a better shot than the last one.

Kirby raised his rifle and fired.

Wheeler watched as Walt crumpled to the ground a mere fifty yards in front of the cabin.

Kirby watched the fuse burn down and sputter into nothingness. No explosion, no destruction, no dead Walt.

Wheeler had fooled them both.

"Why'd you shoot me, Kirby? I was almost there. You had time to stop the dynamite from exploding," gasped Walt.

"Sorry about that," said Kirby. "I couldn't take the chance that you would get here in time."

Wheeler listened to the outlaws as he tried to clear his head and ready another shot.

Walt said nothing more, and Kirby disappeared behind the wall of the shack.

Wheeler guessed that Kirby had ducked below the windowsill, crouched as low to the ground as possible. He took a second shot in the area where he thought Kirby might be. The wall under the window disappeared, the old, dry boards turned to powdery dust and wood slivers.

There was no sign of movement in the shack.

Wheeler called out, "You best come on out Kirby. You ain't got nowhere to go."

No response.

"I've got plenty of food and water," Wheeler lied.

"There'll be others to come. I can wait you out," he continued.

Wheeler wondered if he had managed to wound Kirby.

"Who are you?" said Kirby from somewhere in the cabin.

"Pinkerton agent," said Wheeler. "On assignment to the U.S. Treasury. You're wanted for robbin' the train of a shipment of money from the San Francisco Mint."

"That was a dirty trick you played on Walt," Kirby said.

"Yours was even dirtier. You should've helped your friend out, Kirby."

"I ain't got any friends—just business partners. He knows how things are. He would've done the same."

"What do you say, Kirby, you gonna let me take you in?" asked Wheeler.

Again, no response.

Wheeler made sure that he had another round ready to go in the Sharps.

"You let me know when you get tired of hiding in that shack," said Wheeler. He took out his pocket watch and placed it open on the top of the boulder.

After fifteen minutes, he shouted to the cabin, "You know Kirby, if I lose my patience, I might just have to lob a stick of dynamite your way to speed things up."

Wheeler heard only silence.

The sun was bright now, and it was getting hot. Wheeler removed his jacket and took a swig of water from his canteen. He squinted into the sun to get a better look at the shack. He saw no movement.

He looked at the pocket watch and saw that another ten minutes had passed.

Wheeler took out his field binoculars from the saddlebag. He scanned the shack for signs of life, but saw no movement. In the blown-out section of wall beneath the windowsill, he saw what seemed to be the brim of a hat lying on the floor. The angle of his view was off, and he couldn't be sure that it was a hat. If he just moved forward a few yards and to the left he might be able to tell for sure what lay on the floor of the cabin.

He raised the barrel of his Sharps and aimed for the right edge of the hole that he had previously busted in the wall. He pulled the trigger, and a second later the first hole had expanded into an even bigger hole.

He looked through the binoculars again and saw that against all odds the shot had moved the object farther out of his sight.

"Dammit Henry, that just made things worse," he said aloud.

If he wanted to see for sure, he would have to creep up for a better view, he thought. There was no way around it.

He took solace in knowing that unless Kirby had another more powerful rifle that he didn't know about, he should be safely out of range.

He reloaded his rifle. If Kirby was still alive he could scurry back to his gun for another shot. He holstered his pistol. It would be of no use this far away.

Wheeler took a deep breath, and hunkering down, he ran to the nearest boulder. Well, so far, so good, he thought, as he arrived at his destination. He rescanned the shack, but still couldn't see anything. Another twenty or twenty-five yards forward and to the left should do it.

He steeled himself for another sprint, and then hunkered down and made a dash to the next boulder.

Almost immediately, he heard a loud explosion and felt his left calf rupture into pain. His leg crumpled, and he pushed with his good right leg causing him to roll to the left. He drew his pistol from its holster, and as he spun, he looked up and behind.

Hatless, Kirby stood atop a large outcropping above Wheeler, his rifle raised to his shoulder. He fired again, and the bullet burst a chunk from the rock next to Wheeler.

For a split second, Kirby and Wheeler locked eyes.

Wheeler saw a sudden recognition in Kirby's face.

"Captain Wheeler!" Kirby gasped.

Kirby shot again and grazed Wheeler's right shoulder.

Wheeler shot twice. The first bullet hit Kirby in his right side, and the second shot traveled harmlessly past the outlaw's head.

Now wounded, Kirby moved back to get out of Wheeler's line of fire.

Wheeler seized the opportunity and hobbled back under the outcropping.

"You damned stupid, old fool," he cursed himself.

He'd fallen for one of the oldest tricks in the book. It had been Kirby's hat all right, but Kirby had left it behind on purpose. Furthermore, he should have been aware of the possibility of an escape tunnel—any respectable miner would have dug one in case he was trapped in his cabin.

Kirby must have come out somewhere behind the rock fall, and then outflanked him by circling the valley under cover of the crags above the valley floor. The trap set, Kirby had kept quiet to entice him to get closer to the cabin and draw him out from under the outcropping.

The wily private had outmaneuvered his old captain, yet again.

Wheeler turned his attention to his wounded leg. A small chunk of his calf was simply gone. Part of the meat had been removed, and the rest had been traumatized. Luckily, no major arteries had been severed, and the bleeding had been partially cauterized by the heat of the bullet.

I've been through worse, he thought.

He tore off a sleeve from his shirt and tied it tight

around the wound. He was in terrible pain.

Next, he peeled back his shirt to reveal his right shoulder. Not a problem, thought Wheeler—barely grazed.

"Hey there, Captain Wheeler," taunted Kirby. "I don't think I'm dreamin', and you ain't a ghost 'cause I saw you bleed. So, how come you ain't dead?"

"You know, Private, all these years I've been askin' myself that, and at first, I chalked it up to pure luck. If that bullet had been a bit closer to my heart, then I'd have been a goner. Or maybe if I'd laid there for a little longer, I would have bled to death. And that train engineer—if he hadn't been such a big man, he might not have covered me up so completely and you would have realized that I was still alive, and then finished me off."

Wheeler shifted his weight to ease the pain in his leg, and then continued, "But, if I'm honest, I have to admit that it was really you, Kirby, who kept me alive. It was knowing that I had some unfinished business with Private Kirby Barksdale that gave me a reason to get up in the mornin'."

"So, how bad are you wounded, Captain?"

"Not bad enough to die anytime soon," said Wheeler.

"Me, either."

"That's too bad," Wheeler said.

"Well, Captain, looks like we're at a standstill," said Kirby.

"Oh, I don't know," said Wheeler, "all of your gang is dead or captured. In my book, that puts *me* ahead of *you*."

A wave of silence settled from above.

Wheeler was about to congratulate himself on delivering an affront to his former private, when he felt the press of a cold steel gun barrel at the base of his skull.

"Not *all* of the gang is dead or captured," said the voice attached to the gun barrel.

✶✶✶

"Sorry, Captain, but it looks like you let down your guard again," said Kirby, who had reunited with his brother.

Danny picked up Wheeler's discarded revolver and stuck it in his waistband.

Aldous stood behind Wheeler, and lifting him under his arms, dragged the Pinkerton agent to the rock wall and propped him up.

"Hey Aldous," Danny said, "Why don't you go check on Walt?"

"You bet," responded Aldous, who, eager to ingratiate himself with the Barksdale brothers, immediately trotted off toward the cabin.

Kirby watched the reprobate deputy bounce across the rock-strewn ground, ten-gallon hat and handlebar mustache heightening his already comically tall shadow.

The older Barksdale spit on the ground, and said "Why'd you bring him along?"

"I didn't have much choice. Truth be told, he brought me along."

"How do you figure?" asked Kirby.

"He broke me out of jail, big brother. I'd be swingin' from a noose if it weren't for him—might swing yet, if we get caught."

"You'll get caught, all right. Just a matter of time," Wheeler said.

Kirby spun toward Wheeler, pointed his finger, and angrily said, "Just you shut your mouth, Captain. You sure won't be doing any catchin'. I got plans for you."

Wheeler said nothing and continued watching and listening to the two brothers.

"You could have killed him, or just left after he sprung you," Kirby said to Danny.

"Well, at first he had me handcuffed to make sure that I didn't do either of those things."

"Guess Aldous has a little more sense than I gave him credit for," said Kirby.

"But after a while, I guess he trusted me and took the cuffs off," continued Danny. "What I really wanted to do was just wash my hands of the whole thing. I didn't want to be in the gang anymore, or even see the money. That's why we took a different trail. I planned to lead Aldous as far away from you and the money as I could, and then take off to start a new life."

"So, why'd you change your mind?" asked Kirby

Danny laughed, "Lucky for you that I did. That's what I say."

"Maybe," mumbled Kirby.

"You know me, Kirby. I got to thinkin' that if a man does another man the kind of favor that changes the direction his life is takin', well then maybe he owes that man. Aldous did me that kind of favor, and I owe him something for it."

Danny slapped Kirby on the shoulder, and said, "So, here we are."

"How much do we owe this lawman for your freedom?" Kirby asked suspiciously.

"Aldous wants Bobby's share."

"Bobby's dead. By all rights, his share should revert to the remaining gang members—that's you and me and Walt. The deputy ain't part of the gang."

"I told him that he could have it, Kirby. It's only one-fifth. You, me, and Walt still got the rest."

The sound of jingling spurs signaled the approaching deputy. Kirby and Danny broke off their conversation.

"Sad news, pards," said Aldous, a tad too happily. "Walt's dead."

"Well then," said Kirby, "nothin' to be done but to divvy up the money and go our separate ways."

"Jesus, Kirby, we got to at least give Walt a burial. He was the only friend you had in the world, so you owe him that."

"I suppose we got long enough to do a burial," conceded Kirby.

Aldous cleared his throat and said, "I think we ought to discuss how we're gonna split up the money, gents."

"Don't worry, lawman, you're gettin' Bobby's share," Kirby said.

"Well, I'd like to bring up a different arrangement," said Aldous.

"What do you mean, 'a different arrangement'?" sneered Kirby.

Danny saw the fire in his brother's eyes, and said to Aldous, "This ain't a good idea, Aldous. We made a deal and I say we stick with that deal."

"Well, hold on," said Aldous, "Let me put this out there. It looks to me like the situation has changed a mite. Now that there's only three of us, it seems only fair that we split up the money into three equal shares."

"You need to stick to the original bargain—if you know what's good for you," said Danny.

"Well, hold on, fellas," said Aldous. "If I hadn't sprung Danny out of jail, and then, if we hadn't happened along when we did, well, who knows where you'd be, Kirby."

With no warning Kirby turned on Aldous and shouted, "You ungrateful snake."

Kirby, who was still cradling his rifle, turned the butt end into a club and smashed Aldous on the bridge of his nose.

A shower of blood streamed from the wound, and the lawman reeled backward from the viciousness of the blow.

Danny, predicting Kirby's next move, tried to grab his enraged brother's arms. Kirby was too quick, however; he shot Aldous twice in the chest. Aldous tumbled onto Wheeler.

The dead deputy's lifeless eyes locked on Wheeler, who said to Danny, "Well, there goes another portion. That brother of yours don't like sharin'."

"Like I said, Captain, I got plans for you," said Kirby.

Danny stood between Kirby and Wheeler. He tried to calm down his brother.

"Whoa, Kirby. That's enough. Leave the captain and let's get while we can."

"Not until I finish what I started back in the war. Captain Henry Wheeler is a dead man, that's for sure."

"Come on Kirby, please. Leave him a canteen and let's get out of this place."

"I can't do that, little brother. I aim to kill Wheeler. I can't rest until I finish the job."

"You can have all of the money, if you leave the captain alive," blurted Danny.

Kirby looked stunned. "After all we been through, you're just givin' it all up? I can't believe my own brother could be so yellow and weak."

"I don't want the money any more Kirby. It ain't worth it. It cost a lot of lives."

"That's right, Danny, it cost a lot of lives, and that's *why* it's worth so much. And ain't nobody standin' between me and that money."

"Please, Kirby, just leave the captain be. Take the money and go someplace far away."

"That's the problem, little brother. As long as Captain Wheeler's still alive, there ain't no place far enough away. He'll just keep comin.'"

"Don't do it, Kirby. I've had enough killin' to last me to the end of time. First the war, then the robbin'—and then the killin' that goes along with the robbin'. It's just too much. No more, Kirby. I'm beggin' you. Take your money and go."

"Just one more dead man. This one's real special. I'll leave after I finish him off.

"If you want, you can leave now," Kirby offered.

"Listen, Kirby. I ain't beggin'; now I'm tellin.' No more," warned Danny.

"Get out of my way," Kirby said, as he batted Danny to the side with his rifle. Danny fell to the ground beside Kirby, and Kirby raised the rifle, taking aim at Wheeler.

"I'm beginning to believe that you only shoot unarmed men, Kirby," Wheeler taunted.

Kirby sneered at Wheeler and tensed his trigger finger. Danny anticipated his brother's trigger pull, and, lying on his back, drew his pistol and shot twice. The bullets struck Kirby in the center of the chest forcing him to jerk the rifle barrel upward. Kirby's bullet hit the rock wall above Wheeler.

Kirby fell backward, and Danny rushed to his fallen brother.

"I'm sorry, Kirby. I truly am, but I couldn't let you do it."

Kirby said nothing. He looked at his brother. He motioned for him to come closer.

Danny cradled Kirby's head in his arm and leaned in.

"What happened Danny? You used to look up to me," said Kirby.

"You just made it harder and harder to do," replied Danny.

"When we was boys we were always together. Wherever you found one Barksdale boy, well, the other couldn't be far behind", Kirby said.

"And I've been followin' you ever since."

"Even so," said Kirby, "we was like oil and water, like light and dark. We never did agree on much."

"Yeah, but we was brothers and I always loved you."

Kirby smiled weakly, and whispered to Danny, "Cain and Abel was brothers, and look where that got them."

Kirby's breathing became so shallow and weak that Danny had to put his ear right next to Kirby's lips to hear him say, "You know, little brother, you'll never get to spend that money 'cause it's cursed with the blood of Cain and Abel."

Kirby grew silent. Danny no longer felt the warm air of his brother's breath on his face. He closed Kirby's eyes and gently lowered his dead brother's head to the ground. Slowly he stood, his mind numb with shock, sadness, and guilt.

"I'm gonna need you to put down your weapon," Wheeler said to Danny, as he leveled the dead deputy's pistol at the remaining Barksdale brother.

Wheeler poked the cheery little fire burning in the fireplace. The night had been cold and he had slept fitfully, despite the fact that Danny slept handcuffed and securely tied to the bunk beds on the other side of the room.

It had rained hard starting around midnight and had kept up until almost daylight. This had only increased Wheeler's insomnia.

Yet, the rain and the new morning raised his spirits. He was alive and in reasonably good shape. All of the gang was accounted for, and in a few more hours he would be in possession of the stolen money.

The railroad, the U.S. Treasury, and most importantly, Allan Pinkerton, would never know just how close he had come to losing everything.

Wheeler finished his breakfast, and then changed the dressing on his leg. He whistled a happy tune as he crammed Aldous's star and his belongings into the saddlebag.

"Sure you don't want nothin' to eat?" he asked Danny.

Danny said nothing.

The Pinkerton agent said to his prisoner, "Remember our deal, now. You take me to the cave where the money is hid, and when we get back to Tucson, I recommend that you get a lenient sentence for savin' my life and givin' up the money. I guarantee that they'll listen to me. You won't do no more than five years in prison—you mind your Ps and Qs and you could get out sooner on parole.

You're still a young man, Danny. You got your whole life ahead of you."

"Let's get this over with," said Danny.

★★★

They rode in silence.

Kirby's death had taken all the fight from Danny, and Wheeler had removed the handcuffs. The horses leisurely walked along the trail as it descended to lower ground. The noonday sun was directly overhead. The trail was dry now, last night's downpour just a memory.

A dirt road crossed the path. Danny pointed west and said, "That road takes you back into the desert, and then to the railroad. We gotta go the opposite direction."

He charted an easterly course along the road, doubling back into the heart of the mountains. The road was wide, and Wheeler saw ruts in the ground where a wagon had previously travelled. He looked for hoof prints to get an idea of how many horses had gone up and down this road before, but the rain had obliterated any traces.

They continued in silence until the road dead-ended into a dense thicket of brush in front of a rock wall.

"Almost there," said Danny. "We gotta walk from here."

Wheeler looked at his shot-up leg and asked, "No way to ride on in?"

"Nope, time to dismount. It's a short walk from here."

Barksdale hopped down from his horse and waited as Wheeler gingerly got off his mount and propped himself up on his makeshift crutch.

Danny walked up to the brush on the right and pushed it aside. He moved into the thicket with a rustling noise.

"Come on, Captain," he said, "you want to recover the money, you best get a move on."

Wheeler drew his pistol and warily followed the outlaw into the brush. In front of him he saw a darkened tunnel proceeding into the rock face. Danny entered and Wheeler followed. The tunnel looked to go about thirty yards into the mountain, and then exited into bright sunshine.

The two men walked to the other side of the passageway and came out into a small box canyon. Fallen rock littered the canyon floor, and several small caves were situated at various heights along the walls of the canyon.

"This way," said Danny as he strode to the left side of the canyon, making his way to one of the cave entrances.

Wheeler struggled to keep pace on his injured leg.

"Hold up, wait for me," said Wheeler.

Danny and Wheeler entered the cave entrance side by side. The cave floor was smooth. It looked as if running water, long ago, had polished it clean.

Danny walked to a rock shelf and held up an unlit torch in the dim light. Wheeler took a match out of his shirt pocket and lit it. The light of the flames flickered on the cave walls.

"Follow me," Danny said.

They rounded a bend in the cave and went deeper into the mountain until the cave opened into a larger cavern.

Danny stopped short. He held the torch at arm's length in front of him to force light farther into the cave.

Without warning, he sprinted into the cavern, easily leaving the Pinkerton agent behind. Wheeler held up his pistol and considered whether to shoot Danny, when the outlaw dropped the torch and fell to his knees.

Wheeler walked to where Danny had crumpled.

His gun still drawn, he said, "If this is a trick, Danny, then our deal's off. I'll make sure you get the noose."

"He done it again," said Danny. "Even dead and gone, he's still cursing me."

"What are you talkin' about? Let's keep goin'," said Wheeler.

"Don't you see, Captain? There ain't no goin' on."

Danny looked at Wheeler and said, "All the money's gone."

Wheeler picked up the torch and hobbled forward waving the light from side to side to get a better look. He searched for any sign of boxes, sacks, saddlebags, or piles of bills.

To the left was nothing, and to the right was nothing.

Wheeler turned back to Danny and said, "Are you sure this is the right cave?"

"Of course I'm sure," said Danny. "He moved the money somewhere else after we robbed the train. There was a wagon's worth of money in this cave.

Wheeler had no reason to doubt Danny's assessment of the situation. Danny would surely die if the Pinkerton agent refused to vouch for his cooperation in recovering the money. Besides, Danny was clearly a beaten man who seemed to have no further capacity for trickery or defiance.

"Where do you think he might have moved it?" Wheeler asked.

"How would I know? You saw how many caves are in this canyon. It could be in any one of them, or it could be in another cave in a different canyon. There are hundreds of big and little caves all over this part of the mountains."

Wheeler had a sinking feeling in the pit of his stomach as he contemplated his future with the agency, should he be unable to recover the money.

He peered into the cavern for one last look before they

began the only other course of action left open to them—to search every last cave in the canyon.

He had taken a couple of steps forward when the light from the torch caused something ahead to sparkle and shine. His leg throbbed mercilessly as he limped to the firefly glint that beckoned him.

A small pile of rocks had been fashioned on the cave floor. On top of the cairn, he found what he sought. Wheeler stood over the bauble for at least a minute, afraid to move. Danny had quietly crept beside him and now both men stared in silence. Finally, Wheeler bent over and scooped up the mysterious trinket.

There before the light of the torch, he held up, in front of Danny, a single Indian Head cent. Wheeler turned the coin over in his hand, mesmerized by its brilliance. It looked brand new and polished.

He put on his reading glasses and inspected the copper coin. On the obverse side, he noted the bust of an Indian wearing a headdress. The words 'United States of America' circled the bust, and below it was stamped the date, 1882.

Wheeler flipped the coin over and examined the reverse side. An oak wreath and shield ran along the circumference of the coin and the 'One Cent' denomination was struck in the center. He squinted to find the mintmark. He ran his thumb over the tiny 'S' that signified the San Francisco mint.

Next, he turned his attention to a small folded piece of notepaper that had been placed under the penny.

He unfolded the paper and held it up to the light. In printed lettering, written in pencil, he mouthed the letters on the note.

"I.O.U," it read.

18

Wheeler's leg hurt.

The preacher was of the long-winded variety. Maybe the widow was paying by the word, or maybe the preacher simply wanted to make sure that all within earshot got a good dose of prairie religion before returning to their hardscrabble existences. Brother Broward—he was sure that was what the widow had called the man—looked to be more farmer than man of God.

He hadn't seen such a skinny specimen since his prison days during the tail end of the war. A scare-crow dressed in overalls, a floppy hat and clod hoppers, the parson droned on and on until finally, Wheeler heard the one word that might possibly permit him to sit—'Amen'.

The widow tossed a handful of red dirt into the hole where her husband nestled snuggly in his final pinewood bed. The two little tow headed boys copied their mother and threw tiny fistfuls of dirt into the stiff Oklahoma Territory wind. It flew back at them and dusted their hair and faces.

The widow, who years earlier may have been pretty, squinted into the sun and brushed her dirty blond hair out of her eyes. She pushed a coin into the palms of the two men who had been hired to fill in the grave, and gave two coins and a jar of jam to the preacher, who shook her hand.

"I'll have the missus check in on you and the young'uns

in a day or two," he said to her. He turned and walked away from the grave and the sod house in the direction of his horse and wagon.

She thanked the preacher again and motioned to Wheeler to follow her into the house. The two boys tagged along behind.

Wheeler walked around the freshly dug grave and the two older graves of Emma, aged two and Kirby, aged five. The cracked wooden crosses leaned toward the house. Just nine years had passed since the 1889 Land Run and already three dead. This hard land was an unforgiving place.

The widow, who stood less than five feet tall, and her boys walked through the door upright. Wheeler ducked as he limped across the threshold. He navigated down three steps into the house that was partially dug beneath the ground.

A journey of three small steps plunged him from harsh sunlight to subterranean darkness. A lamp sitting on a table dimly lit the interior of the sod house. He struggled to make his old eyes adjust to the darkness. It was a short trip from here to the grave, thought Wheeler.

A bed lay against one wall and a chest of drawers sat along another. Shelves and alcoves had been dug into the dirt walls and an iron stove sat at the far end of the house, its rickety stovepipe extending through the roof. Various implements, tools, and family belongings hung from the ceiling.

Wheeler took off his hat and held it in his hands. He wiped the sweat from his forehead. The house smelled of damp dirt and dry grass. The temperature was surprisingly cool.

"Have a seat, Captain Wheeler," said the widow.

"It's just Wheeler, I haven't been a captain for a very long time," he said as he pulled out a chair and sat at the small table.

"You can call me Henry, if you want, ma'am," he continued.

Unblinking, she stared at him, before she replied, "Can I get you a drink, Captain Wheeler?"

"I'm fine," he said.

"You still a Pinkerton?" she asked.

"Not a captain, nor a Pinkerton agent," Wheeler answered.

"Once a skunk, always a skunk," she said.

Without acknowledging the slight, he said, "I'm sorry for your loss, ma'am."

"Are you now?" she said. She continued to stand.

He thought he detected the slightest Irish accent.

One of the boys, the smaller of the two, padded over to Wheeler and hugged him. He laid his head against Wheeler's side and sucked a dirty thumb.

"Not a soul in the world to grieve over Danny's grave 'cept for me and the boys. No kin, no friends, not even a dog."

"Danny gets sick and tells me, if somethin' bad happens, to make sure and find Captain Wheeler.

"How will I find this Captain Wheeler? I says.

"Through the railroad, he says.

"What if he don't come, I says.

"He'll come, he says."

All eyes were on Wheeler now.

"Well I'm here," he said. "I'll tell you the truth, there was no love lost between your Danny and me. But, in the end, he was a good man who did the right thing and I owe him my life. So, when I say that I'm sorry for your loss, I truly am."

Danny's widow crossed her arms and said, "Well, I reckon you got one thing right—deep down, Danny was a good man whose only fault was that he loved a bad brother."

Wheeler cleared his throat and said, "Beggin' your pardon, ma'am, but Danny wasn't no saint. He done some bad and he done some good, but, like I said, in the end he did his best to set things right. He did the honorable thing and I respect that."

Wheeler broke off the boy's hug and gently pushed him back toward his mother.

"And you're forgettin' the most important thing," he said.

"I let Danny go—*at considerable cost to myself.*"

She abruptly turned and walked to the stove. She reached up to a shelf and took down a little tin box. Returning to the table, she opened the box and brusquely tossed the contents onto the table.

A tarnished, 1882 Indian Head penny bounced on the tabletop. Wheeler picked it up and rubbed it between his thumb and forefinger. It was cold to the touch like the dead men who had coveted it and its kind. He turned it over and felt the 'S' engraved beneath the oak wreath.

Danny's widow crossed her arms and puffed herself up. She scowled at Wheeler.

"Danny said to give you this," said the widow.

"Now get out."

EPILOGUE

San Francisco - 1910

Wheeler's leg hurt. Wheeler's back hurt. Wheeler's stomach hurt. Wheeler's mind hurt. Wheeler's soul hurt.

The years had not been kind to Henry Wheeler. The world had not been kind to Henry Wheeler.

Henry had been born in 1830 on a small southern Virginia plantation. His family had not owned slaves, but he had only known the world of 'King Cotton' and all that that entailed. He had seen his world turned upside down when the South lost the war. There was nothing left for Henry to go back to. So, when Allan Pinkerton took him under his wing, he had enthusiastically left the South behind and had embraced the new world of 'progress' and manifest destiny. America had advanced from a sleepy, isolated former colony to a vibrant, turbulent, continent-sized ball of energy.

At first, when he was younger, change had been invigorating, but as he grew older it became dizzying and bewildering. He had seen too much. He tallied up the developments in his mind—steam power, abolition, locomotives, railroads from the Atlantic to the Pacific, the taming of the West, motor cars, the telephone, electrification, radio, moving pictures, and even flight. People now dared to question the most basic of assumptions—the nature of the races, the nature and origins of mankind, a woman's place in society, why, even some had dared question the existence of God.

He had seen loved ones and enemies die, presidents come and go, fortunes made and lost. Henry had seen his own circumstances progress from bright and boundless to faltering, stagnant, and dismal. In short order, he had lost his position with the Pinkerton Agency, succumbed to drink, seen his marriage fail, presided over the demise of his own detective agency, lost a daughter, contributed mightily to the failure of a second marriage, and eventually was reduced to poverty, ill health, and bitterness.

Even his beloved adopted city of San Francisco had been shaken to the core by a massive earthquake and fires, and was, even now, in the process of changing into an unrecognizable place.

Henry used to wonder why people had to die, but now he knew. People grew old and died because they were no longer able to deal with change. It was both a way to remove impediments to progress and a means to relieve the mental and emotional trauma of those who refused to evolve.

And why couldn't people adapt to change? Because each of us believes that the world of our prime is the best, the greatest, the *only* world there is. Why would anyone want to change something that's already perfect?

As he stood on the sidewalk of a fashionable San Francisco street, he marveled at the journey that had brought him to this time and place. Henry realized that he had become unmoored from his past, and he drifted, lost in an uncharted present. He was, quite simply, an old man seeking confirmation that his past had had some meaning and, just a bit, of value.

Henry gazed at the steps leading up to the mansion. It would be a long trip just climbing to the front door. He raised his foot and placed it on the step, braced himself with his cane, and pushed down until he stood with both feet firmly planted on the bottom step.

The final journey begun at last, he thought.

He had written to the owner of the mansion a year ago, asking for a meeting. He had received no response so he asked again, and again, and again, and again—until finally, Henry had been invited to tea.

Eight small treks later, Henry arrived at the top of the stairs and knocked on the ornate front door. The door opened, and a butler greeted him. Henry gave the butler his invitation, and the dour man showed him to a seat in the foyer.

"Please, follow me to the library, Captain Wheeler," the butler said, upon his return.

It had been ages since anyone had addressed him as Captain Wheeler, thought Henry, wistfully.

He slowly followed the butler past a grand sweeping staircase to a set of double doors, off the side of the foyer. The butler opened the doors and gestured for Wheeler to enter the book-filled room.

Wheeler shuffled in and stood shakily on the threshold. The butler retreated and shut the doors behind him.

Wheeler smiled and said, "Hello Mrs. Holcomb. Or, should I call you Maggie?"

★★★

The woman sat in a brocade chair next to the fireplace. A young man stood behind her, serving as bodyguard. A large oil painting of an older distinguished-looking man hung above the fireplace.

She noticed Henry gazing at the painting, and said, "My late husband, Mr. Holcomb."

Wheeler's bones ached and his feet and hands were cold. His entire body called out for the little fire that merrily burned across the room.

"Won't you come sit by me, next to the fire, Captain Wheeler?"

"Thank you, Mrs. Holcomb. I won't lie, ma'am. The warmth will be a relief to my old bones," he said. "By the way, please call me Henry."

She patted the chair next to her, and said, "Please, Henry, sit here."

She smiled back at him.

"Mrs. Holcomb is so formal. Call me Maggie," she continued.

Henry took his seat and stretched out his tired legs.

He took in the woman who sat next to him, sizing her up like the old detective that he was. Graying black hair piled high in the pompadour style made fashionable by the illustrations popularly known as the *Gibson Girls*. Her dress was richly detailed silk, modestly tailored as befit her age. A long string of pearls hung around her neck and matched her pendant earrings. A brightly colored cloisonné brooch in the shape of a peacock was pinned to the bodice of her dress.

An old scar marred her forehead.

Still a fine-looking woman, thought Wheeler.

"Would you like a cup of tea, Henry? Or, if you prefer, I can have something stronger brought in."

"Tea's fine. I gave up the other a long time ago," said Wheeler.

Wheeler looked at the young man standing behind Maggie.

"Hello, Captain Wheeler," he said.

Wheeler took the cup of tea from Maggie, and said to the young man, "You must be Harry. Is that right?"

"Yes, sir. I'm Harry Holcomb."

Wheeler judged Harry to be in his early thirties. He was tall and lean with a hairless face and freckles. His red hair was short and parted in the middle. His expensively tailored suit fit him like a glove. Piercing blue eyes intently watched the old detective.

"I must say that you're the spitting image of your father," said Wheeler.

Harry glanced at his mother and replied, "Looks can be deceiving."

Maggie took a sip of her tea.

"So, Henry, what do you want?"

"Don't really want anything," he said. "Just for you to tell me that I'm right about a few things. You see, I figured out a long time ago that you were the one who got to the money before I did.

"It took me a good part of a lifetime to find you. I knew you would have money, so I looked for a newly rich woman with a little boy. But, I didn't count on you concocting a completely different life.

"It was after the earthquake that I found you. A few wealthy families headed the rebuilding effort, and pictures of you and Harry were in all the newspapers. It was the society pages that nailed it. Seems you also like to donate a lot of time and money to a charitable association for the betterment of fallen women.

"Well, it turns out we were in the same city all along."

He paused.

"Of course, just seein' Harry in the flesh, tells me a

whole lot. And you, a former saloon girl living in the lap of luxury."

"My husband, Mr. Holcomb, was a wealthy man," she said.

"Right, shipping, I'm told. Seems he didn't have a plug nickel before he met you, though. I hear it was your money that provided seed for the business."

Harry reached over to the fireplace and picked up the iron poker. He stirred the fire as Wheeler watched him warily.

"I figure that Levi, being the fool that he was, told you everything you needed to know about where the money was hid. That was the part that you left out of the note. Wasn't it, Maggie?

"You decided to go after the money yourself when Aldous roughed you up and threatened you. Am I right?"

Maggie remained silent.

"So, first thing in the morning, you hightailed it out on the train. You got off at the nearest way station where you rented a wagon and a team of mules. I checked on that Maggie, and the stationmaster told me that a pretty woman and a little boy rented the team for a couple of days. He also said that you purchased some empty barrels. When you returned, the barrels were full and you shipped them to a Mrs. Mary Frazier in St. Louis—it took a lot of digging, but I found out that was where you were originally from.

"I reckon that while the men were killin' each other in the mountains, you and Harry were haulin' out the money.

"You must be a lot tougher than you look, Maggie."

Maggie took another sip of tea, and said, "So, what *proof* do you have that it was *me* who took the money?"

Wheeler reached into his jacket pocket and dropped the contents onto the table. An old deputy's star clattered onto the polished wood, and a tattered and folded piece of paper slid to a stop in front of the teapot.

Maggie picked up the paper, unfolded it and briefly glanced at it.

"That's your daddy's badge," Wheeler said to Harry.

"And, that's your note to Aldous, telling him about the Barksdale gang at the saloon and their hidden money," he said to Maggie. "After Kirby gunned down Aldous, I gathered up his belongings, and I found the note in his pocket."

"Fine, but that doesn't prove it was me who took the stolen money—only that I told Aldous about it."

Wheeler reached into the other pocket and pulled out another folded piece of paper. He opened it and held it up for the mother and son to see.

It was the I.O.U. that he had found in the cave.

"Same paper, same printing, written in pencil. It's your note, Maggie," he said.

Maggie rose from her chair and stood beside her son.

"I suppose you've come to collect," she said.

"Nope, I only want some peace of mind. I just wanted a chance to talk to you."

"You know, Henry, I could simply pay back the money. I have many times more now than what I took," Maggie said.

"No need. I think you've done some real good with your money—more so, than any of us would have done. You did the best you could for your son, your family and your community. You've lived an honorable life, Maggie, and that's the only thing that I have respect for now.

He paused for a second and then said, "You know

Maggie, there is something you could do for me. Danny had a widow and a couple of boys out in the old Oklahoma Territory. I don't know what happened to them, or if they're even alive, but, it would go a long ways toward makin' things right if you could help them out."

Wheeler slowly stood.

"I should be going, now," he said. "It's been a pleasure meetin' you both. Thank you for seein' me."

"The pleasure was all mine, Henry."

Harry shook Wheeler's hand.

"Good day, sir," Harry said.

Maggie rang for the butler, who promptly entered the room.

"James, help Captain Wheeler down the steps," she said.

The butler held Wheeler under the elbow to steady him.

"Oh, I almost forgot," said Wheeler. "I want to give you something, Harry."

Wheeler held out his hand and Harry held out his open palm.

As Maggie watched, Henry dropped an old, worn Indian Head penny into her son's hand.

Without another word Henry turned and left with the butler.

The library door closed behind Wheeler leaving Maggie and Harry alone by the fire.

Holding up the coin, Harry said, "I believe this should rightfully belong to you, Mother."

"No, Harry, I want you to have it. It was meant as a cruel joke on your father. It was foolish and mean of me. I'm ashamed now to have done it.

"Keep it with you as a reminder of where we come from and how we got to this place. The West is subdued now—less wild. Your father was part of that uncivilized world.

"Remember that when you judge him," she said.

"And Captain Wheeler?" asked Harry.

"Henry Wheeler has one foot in the past and one foot in the present."

"And what about you, Mother? Where do you stand?"

"My, my," scolded Maggie, "this conversation has grown too serious.

"You, my boy, why your path clearly lies in the future. That is what I would much prefer to talk about. We have so many plans for this great city of ours."

Maggie took her son by the arm and led him to a big bay window. As they surveyed the San Francisco skyline and talked of the future, Captain Henry Wheeler slowly limped away.

Rattletrap

Joe Russo surveyed the tavern for money-making opportunities. The whole establishment was dirty, grimy, and rundown. The bartender looked like an old baked potato left in the oven too long, and the only other customer, an ancient, skinny rummy, propped herself against the back wall like a strip of peeling paint.

He'd already checked the bathroom looking for someone to roll—nada, zip. If he didn't find a rube soon, he'd be scouring the sidewalks for old cigarette butts and lost change.

The fan behind the bar whirred and hummed, making him sleepy. He took a gulp of his lukewarm beer and would have spit it out if not for the fact that it might be the last one he drank for a long time. At least the bar was dark and cool. The sun at eleven in the morning was already unbearable. St. Louis, Oklahoma City, Albuquerque, and now Phoenix. It just kept getting hotter. He had chosen this bar stool precisely because it was situated directly in front of the only fan.

The spinning fan blades reminded him of the propellers on the big lumbering B-17s that he'd fueled and cleaned during the war. Man, what a crummy job that had been. A full crew of ten men might leave, and only one or two would return. It had been his job to scrub out the blood, guts, and leftover body parts before they patched up the bird for another mission.

"Hey, Russo," the ground crew would say, "After you finish scrubbing out my plane, I got some toilets need cleanin'."

The bombers would come limping in from a bombing raid over Germany, all shot to hell. Some would barely make it, and some would crash and burn on their own turf. You survive the worst pounding imaginable only to die at the last moment trying to land. What a way to leave this world, he thought.

Not him, he was no hero. He'd dodged the draft for almost a year after Pearl, hiding out in Chicago pool halls, bars, and betting parlors, and then—Bam! His own pop turns him in. Before he knows it, he's in England, stranded on some airfield in the middle of nowhere. He'd just gotten out of the brig for what must have been the twentieth time—truth was he'd spent most of his time in England either locked up or doing crap duty for crimes he'd committed—and the captain says, "Russo, I finally found a way to get rid of your ass. I'm shippin' you off to Italy and the Fifteenth Air Force. You can raise hell and lollygag on some other poor sap's watch. Now you're someone else's problem. "

After one month at Bari Airfield, he'd gone AWOL.

Italy was a mess. Italians surrendering left and right, some pretending that they'd never been in the war. Mussolini had to be rescued by the Germans and moved up to the north.

Italy was hell for the Italians, but it was a dream come true for an Italian kid from Chicago. Russo spoke the language, and he'd found plenty of ways to make some money. Joe rode out the war in Naples and, like all the other Italians; he pretended that he'd never even heard of the war.

He liked Italy, but it wasn't America, so after the Japanese had surrendered, he'd gotten a fake Italian passport, and when he got a chance, he shipped out on a freighter as a seaman.

Joe snuck back into his own country.

He tried going back to Chicago, but his family wouldn't have anything to do with him, and his friends would just as soon turn him in for desertion as look at him. He'd been bumming around ever since.

Except for the heat, the southwest suited him. There were fewer nosey cops, and people were less likely to know anyone from the old neighborhood.

Joe downed the last of his beer. He reached into his pocket and searched for some change. The cost of another drink would almost tap him out. Oh, well, he thought, as he ordered another beer, I'd rather drink than eat.

Joe took a sip of the cold beer, congratulating himself on making a fine business decision, when he noticed a dirty, rusty pickup truck pull up to the curb across the street.

An old-timer in a checked shirt and dusty dungarees got out. He wore boots on his feet and a stained Fedora on his head. His hair and beard were snowy white.

A mongrel terrier yapped from the front seat. The old man held the door open, and the dog jumped to the street. The man and his dog entered a small grocery store.

The bartender passed by, and Joe asked, "Who's the old coot?"

"Old prospector," said the bartender.

"You mean like with a shovel and pickaxe looking for gold and silver? They still got those in 1947?"

"That's right, mister. He lives out in Vulture City. He

works the old Vulture Mine. It played out years ago, and they closed it in forty-two. He's not supposed to be in there, but the town's abandoned, like the mine, so there's nobody around to keep him out."

"You're shittin' me," said Joe. "The guy lives in a ghost town and looks for gold in a place called the Vulture Mine?"

The bartender laughed and said, "You're not from around here are you, mister? This part of Arizona has lots of old ghost towns and abandoned mines."

He paused and said, "And lots of crazy old prospectors."

The bartender put some bottles of Budweiser into the refrigerator behind the bar. Joe drank his beer and watched as the old man and the dog led a stock boy to the back of the truck where he loaded the groceries.

They went back into the store.

Joe said to the bartender, "Man, that's a lot of food."

"Gotta last him at least a couple of months. He doesn't come to town very often."

"So, he lives out in the desert for months at a time by himself?

"Yep."

"His name's Mike," the bartender said.

"Does he have any family?"

"Used to."

"Not no more, huh?"

"His wife ran off with a guy who used to own a gasoline distributorship."

"What do you mean *used to own*?" asked Joe.

"He's a Jap. When the war broke out, they sent him and his new wife to an internment camp up in Washington state. Mike offered to take her back, but she says she'd rather go to a prison camp than come back to him. By the time the war was over they'd lost the business. They resettled somewhere in California."

"Man, that's cold—his wife running off like that. I feel for the old guy," said Joe.

"Even worse," continued the bartender, "Mike's son joined the Navy, and his ship was torpedoed by the Japs. So then, his wife and his son are both gone. He's all alone, just him and his mangy dog. He blames the Japs—wants to kill 'em all."

"Of course," said Joe. "Who can blame him?"

Joe watched the old man return with another load of supplies.

"All that grub must cost a fortune," Joe said.

"Mike's got plenty of money. He brings in some gold to the assayer's office every few months and gets cash to buy his supplies. The banker's been trying for years to talk Mike into opening an account. The crazy fool says his money is safer hidden out in the desert."

Joe's ears pricked up.

"I thought you said that the mine was played out."

"It's rumored that Mike found an overlooked vein of gold—not enough to reopen the mine, but more than enough for one man."

Suspiciously, the bartender said, "Say, you sure are asking a lot of questions. You want to know so much, why don't you go and ask Mike yourself?"

Joe watched the prospector and his dog get into the truck.

Joe gulped down his beer, grabbed his duffel bag, and ran for the exit, shouting, "Thanks, I will."

✳✳✳

The car horn startled Mike. He turned his head to see a tall, swarthy man dodge a Buick and run toward his truck.

"Hey, mister, do you have some spare change?" said Joe.

Joe placed himself in front of the truck's bumper, preventing Mike from leaving.

Mike's dog barked at the man and growled low.

"Please, mister. I haven't eaten in a couple of days. I just need a little money for food."

"I don't give charity to bums," Mike said. "Besides, I just saw you drinking your lunch in the bar."

"A beer's cheaper than a meal," Joe said. "I'm having a little trouble adjusting to civilian life since I came back from the Pacific."

Mike paused and eyed Joe up and down, trying to take stock of his character.

"Hard to hold down a regular job when all you're used to is sleeping in the jungle and killing Japs."

Mike stopped short of turning the truck's ignition.

"Where'd you fight, son?" he asked.

"You name it," said Joe. "Philippines, Guam, Okinawa, Iwo. Anywhere the Marines told me to go, I gladly went. Anywhere Japs needed killing," he lied.

"My son died at Midway," said Mike.

"I'm sorry for your loss. I'm sure he died a hero, sir," Joe said, as he held out his hand to Mike.

Mike and Joe shook hands.

"I'm Joe Russo."

The old prospector hesitated before he said, "Mike. I'm Mike Baxter."

"Like I was saying, Mike, I just need something temporary so I can get on my feet enough to finish my journey to California. I've got an uncle there—Uncle Carmine—who's got a job waiting for me."

"You're not from around here, are you, Joe?" said Mike.

"No sir, I'm from Chicago originally. But after the war, well, Chicago is just too big for me. I want to start some place fresh. You know, some place a man can stretch out."

Joe sensed that Mike was judging him so he said, "In the cities, people are suspicious of each other. They're quick to judge and slow to lend a hand. That's what I like about the West—people look out for one another."

"Where is your family from, Joe?" asked Mike.

"From Chicago, sir. Like I said."

"No," said Mike, "I mean what country did your family come from? You're kind of dark complected."

"Oh, I see what you're getting at. My family is from Italy."

"I see," said Mike.

"That's on my father's side. On my mother's side, well, her family goes all the way back to the Mayflower. I believe some of her people even fought in the War for Independence. So, you see, I come from a long line of soldiers," said Joe.

"Um-hmm," said Mike."

Joe sensed a big fish getting away. So, he tried to reel the old man in.

"Of course, my mom died while I was away in the war so she never got to see me come home."

Both men grew silent for a moment, and then Joe said, "So, Mike, if you don't have any work for me, could you give me a ride to get me a little farther down the road?"

The old man stroked his beard and said, "I suppose I could do that. I can only take you as far as Vulture City.

By the time we get there, it will be about dark. I'll give you some supper, and you can sleep in a bed. I'm sure that would be a welcome change."

"Yes, sir, you bet it would. Thanks, Mike. I really appreciate it."

"Now remember, just for the night. You can share some breakfast with me, and then you need to be on your way before I start my workday."

"I won't be any trouble. I promise," said Joe.

"Well, get in," said Mike.

✶✶✶

The drive to Vulture City was long, hot, and dusty. The two men hadn't talked much. Joe had asked Mike if he could turn on the radio, and Mike had said sure, but when Joe reached over to turn it on, the dog—which Mike had introduced as Sweetie—had bitten his hand. Mike thought it was the funniest thing that he'd ever seen, and Joe pretended to laugh, too—even though he really wanted to strangle the dog and Mike, too.

They had to stop once for gas and Mike bought Joe a Coke while the attendant filled the tank and saw to the truck. The two men talked as they sipped their Cokes.

"What kind of job does your Uncle Carmine have for you?" Mike asked.

Joe thought quickly and said the first thing that popped into his head. "Working in a kitchen. Uncle Carmine owns a restaurant. He promised to teach me to be a real Italian cook."

"A restaurant, say that's a real coincidence. I own a restaurant too," said Mike.

"I thought you said you're a prospector."

"I am. I got a restaurant in Vulture City—just no

customers on account that it's a ghost town."

"I don't understand," said Joe. "Why'd you get a restaurant in Vulture City?"

"I grew up in Vulture City. The restaurant belonged to my dad, and I got it when he died.

"Vulture City wasn't always a ghost town. When I was a kid, about five thousand people lived there. We lived above the restaurant—I still do. That's where we're going now. Things were good until the gold played out and people started losing their jobs at the mine."

As the men spoke, Mike bent down to pet the dog, and Joe noticed a necklace made of something that looked like old, calloused fingers.

"What's that around your neck?" he asked.

"My good luck charms," said Mike. "It's a necklace made out of the rattles of rattlesnakes that I've killed. I fill them with BBs to keep them rattling."

"That must have taken a long time to get that many rattles," said Joe.

"Not really. The land around Vulture City is full of rattlers. When I was a kid, the town used to have an annual rattlesnake hunt because so many people had died from their bites."

"I don't like snakes," said Joe. "They give me the willies."

"They're not so bad. I trust them more than most people."

Mike paid for his gas and they continued their journey.

Soon, the wind, the heat and the bouncing of the old truck had put Joe to sleep.

He awoke to the sound of the dog barking.

"Well, home sweet home," said Mike.

The truck barreled down a dirt road. Old houses in

various states of disrepair lined both sides of the road. Mike turned left at a ramshackle filling station and took another dirt road until he came to an old paved road that was full of potholes. The road sign read, 'Main Street'.

The old man took a right and maneuvered his way through the sand-filled craters in the pavement.

Joe looked in wonder at the rundown businesses and houses. The buildings were falling apart, but it looked like the owners had just left without bothering to pack up or salvage anything of value.

"Lots of valuable stuff just lying about," said Mike. "Whenever I need something to repair my home, I just rummage around town for spare parts—nine times out of ten I can find what I need."

He laughed and said, "That's one of the advantages of living in a ghost town."

Mike steered the truck to a stop in front of a building on which the word 'Restaurant' was painted.

Joe got out of the truck and retrieved his duffel bag from the back. He waited for Mike and his dog to come around.

Mike led the way into the restaurant, and Joe followed.

"I'll show you to your room, and we can get started on supper," said Mike. "I go to bed as soon as it gets dark, and I wake up as soon as it gets light."

Joe couldn't help noticing that the wallet in Mike's back pocket was bulging.

✲✲

It turned out Mike was a pretty good cook. Hash had never tasted so good.

Joe really hadn't eaten in a couple of days—one of the few things that he hadn't lied about. He cleaned his plate and Mike offered him seconds, which Joe gratefully accepted.

Mike asked Joe about his experiences in the war, and Joe artfully wove a story from newsreels, hearsay, and real people that he'd known in the service. The old man asked Joe about Chicago and his Italian family, and Joe told him the truth—more or less.

Joe asked Mike about growing up in Vulture City and about the old days, but when he tried to steer the conversation to Mike's family or the gold mine, the old man dodged the questions with a skill that impressed the young grifter.

The conversation petered out, and just as Mike had said, he announced that it was time for bed as the sunlight waned.

Joe thanked Mike again for the dinner and the bed and went to his room.

"I'll be up shortly," said Mike. "I let Sweetie out at night to play with the coyotes."

"OK, Mike. Thanks again," Joe said as he shut the bedroom door.

He lay on his back on the bed with his clothes on and his hands behind his head. Mike and the dog went down the stairs and Joe heard the door open and shut as the dog was let out for the night.

He heard Mike come back upstairs and go into his room across the hall and shut the door. The only two residents of Vulture City had settled down for the night. Mike stared at the ceiling and listened intently to the sounds of the old building.

He tried to count the coyotes howling in the distance, but soon gave up. He listened for a dog's howl, but heard none.

They probably sound the same, he thought.

The desert wind picked up as the night progressed, and the old restaurant sang a sad creaking and groaning song in the night.

Joe couldn't stop thinking about Mike's cash-filled wallet. The bartender had said that Mike refused to put any of his money in a bank. It was all hidden somewhere along with the gold that the old prospector had mined. The wallet was probably just a small bit of the fortune that Mike had squirreled away over the years.

The old man grunted and coughed for what seemed like ages.

Joe had pawned his watch in Oklahoma City. He tried to guess the time.

When did it get dark, and when could he expect the sun to come up, he wondered?

Joe got out of bed and paced the room. The floor creaked. He hoped that Mike couldn't hear him walking back and forth.

Despite some reservations, Mike had fallen for his bull-shit story about the Japs. Some people sure were dumb, thought Joe. A guy like Mike deserved to get taken to the cleaners.

But then again, he was really a nice old guy when you got to know him. He had fed Joe a good meal and given him a warm bed to sleep in. He could have just left him standing in front of the bar. Besides, he thought, he really did get a bum deal, what with his wife leaving and his son dying at sea.

Joe stopped his pacing and listened carefully. He heard snoring. Deep, loud, persistent snoring was coming from Mike's room. The old man was sawing logs. It sounded like he was really out cold.

What time did the sun come up? He guessed around five in the morning. Mike had said that he was up with the sun. Joe guessed that it was now around ten at night.

Mike had been nice, but Joe really needed that money. If he took the wallet and left now, then he would be long gone before Mike woke up and got in the truck to look for him.

Better yet, Joe thought, I'll get the keys and take the truck too. That way, Mike couldn't come after him.

Without really knowing it, Joe had talked himself into robbing Mike.

He cracked the door and looked down the hallway. He saw no movement, so he opened the door all the way and listened.

All he heard was Mike's snoring.

Joe tiptoed to Mike's door and listened some more. He opened the door and peeked inside the room.

Mike lay on his bed in pajamas. A window was open beside the bed, and the curtains billowed gently in the breeze.

Joe slowly opened the door all the way and stood silently in the doorway ready to bolt should Mike stir. After a while, he entered a couple of feet into the room and carefully looked around.

Mike's clothes lay over the back of a chair. A dresser sat against a wall and a Zenith Bakelite radio sat atop it. A door led into what Joe guessed was a closet.

Mike continued to snore, and Joe, feeling emboldened, walked to the chair. He rummaged through the pants pockets and quickly found the wallet. He opened the wallet to inspect the money.

It was a lot, that was for sure, he thought, but he didn't

dare count it in Mike's room. He would take stock of his takings once he got clear of Vulture City.

He found the truck keys in one of the front pockets and thrust them into his own pants pocket. For good measure, he took the change and chewing gum in the other pocket.

He couldn't believe his good luck.

Time to leave.

He stealthily made his way toward the hallway.

Joe stopped and considered the dresser. He wondered what it held. Probably just socks and underwear—but then again, some people liked to keep valuables or little sentimental trinkets in the dresser drawers, tucked in with the clothes. Maybe some old jewelry, a Zippo lighter, or a pocketknife.

He opened the top drawer, being careful that it didn't stick and make a noise.

Yep, underwear, just as he'd thought.

Joe lifted the clothes to search for anything that might be hidden beneath, when he heard a low growl coming from behind him.

He turned to confront the sound and saw Sweetie's head poking out from underneath Mike's bed.

The damn dog's still in the house, thought Joe.

The dog scooted out from under the bed and barked loudly at the intruder.

Mike sat up in bed, and quickly realizing the situation, reached under his pillow. He leveled a gun at Joe, and simultaneously, Sweetie attacked him.

Mike fired, but missed, the bullet lodging somewhere in the wall next to Joe.

Joe knocked the dresser over onto Sweetie, pinning the dog. He grabbed the first thing at hand and hurled it with all of his might in Mike's direction.

The radio hit Mike in the head, and he fell backward.

Joe rushed Mike and pinned him to the bed. He held Mike's gun hand and with the other hand picked up the radio and bashed Mike on the head.

Mike groaned, and Joe took his gun.

The old man held his bleeding head and said, "What have you done to Sweetie?"

"What was the damn dog doing in the house?" said Joe.

"He wouldn't go outside, so I brought him upstairs with me. Sometimes he sleeps under my bed. He probably smelled a rat. Turns out he was a lot smarter than I was," said Mike.

Mike stood and started toward the dresser.

"Stay on that bed," said Joe.

"I want to see if he's all right."

"OK, but I'm watching you," said Joe as he pointed the gun at Mike.

Mike picked up the dresser and set it against the wall.

Sweetie lay on the floor, whimpering.

"I think he's got two broken legs," said Mike. "He needs to see a vet."

"I'm sorry about Sweetie", Joe said. "And about your head, too."

"You needn't be. I would've killed you if I could have. Boy, am I a stupid old man, or what? You really played on my kindness, Joe."

"I told you I needed a little money. You should've helped me back in Phoenix."

"C'mon Joe, it wouldn't have been enough. You would have rolled the next guy you met."

"Shut up, Mike. I told you I was in a jam. I just needed

something to tide me over until I got to California."

"It's never enough for your kind," said Mike. He spat in Joe's face, and Joe backhanded him as hard as he could.

Mike fell to the floor, and Sweetie tried to swim to Mike with his front paws.

"You know, Mike," said Joe, "maybe you're right. The money in this wallet is just chump change, isn't it? The bartender told me that you got money and gold hidden somewhere out here."

Mike said nothing and glared at Joe.

"He said the banker's been trying to get you to put your money in the bank for years. He says that you think it's safer out here with you.

"You're going to show me where your fortune is hidden. When I get it all loaded onto that truck of yours, then I'll have enough—when I take everything from you, then it'll be enough, Mike. How do you like that?"

"I'm not going to show you a damn thing," said Mike.

Joe put his foot over Sweetie and said, "Sure you are."

"I told you, I'm not doing anything that you want," hollered Mike.

Joe pressed on Sweetie's back legs with the bottom of his foot, and the dog let out a hurt yelp.

"Where's it hidden Mike? In the restaurant?"

Joe stepped on Sweetie again, this time harder. The dog's anguished cries were more than Mike could take.

"It's all hidden in the mine," Mike blurted.

"Good," said Joe, "you're going to take me there tomorrow."

"Fine, but you got to promise me that you'll drop off Sweetie at the nearest vet after you leave. I can last out here by myself for months, but you've got to swear that you'll get my dog patched up."

"No problem. You take me to your money, and I'll take care of your dog."

"It's a deal," said Mike.

✶✶✶

Mike spent a sleepless night tied up in a chair in the restaurant, Sweetie beside him in one of the dresser drawers.

Joe didn't dare sleep, even though Mike was tied up and he now had the gun.

Just as he had figured, the sun rose about five in the morning and Joe rose up, too. He made some coffee. Mike watched as Joe drank.

When he finished, he said, "Listen Mike, you got to do what I say if you want Sweetie to live."

"I'm going to untie you and you're going to drive me to the mine where you'll show me the money."

"What about my dog?" said Mike.

"He stays here while we go to the mine. When I get the money, then we come back here and I take him with me and drop him off at a vet."

Mike nodded in agreement, and Joe untied him and marched him to the truck at gunpoint. Mike got in the driver's side, and Joe went around to the passenger side. He slid in the truck and gave Mike the keys.

"OK, let's go. Straight to the mine and nowhere else," said Mike.

The mine turned out to be just outside the town, maybe a fifteen-minute drive from Mike's restaurant.

Joe saw lots of tools and implements scattered about the entrance to the mine. Some he recognized—pickaxes, shovels, buckets, hammers, and strainers—and lots that he didn't recognize.

Barrels of trash lay around the entrance, too.

"What's with all the trash?" asked Joe.

"I bring it out here to get rid of it."

"Why don't you just burn it like everybody else?"

"Because it's a waste of gasoline," replied Mike. "I just dump it down a big hole in the mine."

Joe kicked over one of the barrels to show Mike that he meant business.

"Let's get going," he said.

Mike led Joe to the entrance.

He picked up an electric lantern.

"Give me one of those," said Joe.

The men switched on their lights and proceeded, Joe covering Mike with the gun.

They followed the gently sloping shaft for a while, until they came to a cross shaft.

Mike stopped and said, "I need to rest a minute. I don't feel well."

"What's wrong?" asked Joe.

"I'm out of breath, and I've got a pain in my chest."

Mike sat down.

"No stopping until we get to the money," said Joe.

"I can't help it. My chest hurts really bad," Mike said, gasping.

The old prospector grabbed his chest and said, "I think I'm having a heart attack."

"A heart attack? Listen to me old man; you can't die on me now. Not before you show me the money."

Joe rushed to Mike's side to try to keep his meal ticket alive. He bent over to judge how badly Mike was hurt.

Mike picked up a rock and smashed it onto Joe's head, sending him reeling backward. He felt the ground give out under his left foot. The sound of breaking boards echoed in the darkness. Loose rocks skittered and rolled under Joe's feet. He dropped his lantern and heard a distant splash.

Joe kept falling backward and was surprised when he landed on his butt with a thud. He had evidently fallen across the corner of a hole and kept going to the other side.

He was alive and on solid ground.

"Serves you right," Mike said, as he scanned the shaft with the light.

Enraged, Joe shot twice at Mike's lantern, and it dropped to the ground.

"Mike. Mike."

Silence.

"Mike, are you OK?"

Joe got up and carefully made his way around the broken boards and the hole in the ground.

The old man lay sprawled on the ground.

Joe checked for a pulse, but found none. Mike was clearly dead.

He rolled Mike to the hole and pushed him in with his feet.

Mike disappeared into the inky hole, and a few moments later his body made a noisy splash.

"Sorry, Mike," said Joe.

Joe picked up Mike's lantern and looked about.

Joe was alone now in a dark passageway with two branching shafts. Which way to go, he wondered?

"I'm sure as hell not turning back now," he said aloud.

He reached into his pocket and pulled out a dime.

"Heads, I go right, and tails I go left."

He flipped the coin into the air and let it drop to the ground.

Tails, he would take the shaft to the left.

Joe traveled on, carefully checking the ground in front of him for more holes. It was slow going. He would shine his light on the ground, and then move a few feet, shine his light farther down the shaft to look for any sign of Mike's money, and then repeat the process.

Finally, he shone his lantern down the shaft and could just make out something in the distance that glittered in the light. He gingerly inched closer figuring that if he were near the money, then Mike would have likely set up some traps.

He moved about twenty-five yards closer to the object that had reflected the light and swung the lantern back and forth. Trapped in the beam of the lantern, Joe saw white tarps with something under them. He stopped and frantically moved the lantern back and forth to catch the scene in the light.

There was something else sitting next to whatever was under the tarps. It looked like barrels. He moved farther down the shaft trying to get the lantern's illumination close enough to see what lay ahead.

Suddenly, he realized what it was.

They were barrels sitting next to the tarps. In the barrels, something sparkled and glittered in the light.

Barrels full of gold! he thought.

No wonder he couldn't take this to a bank. Joe guessed that there must be more barrels under the tarps. He figured that these were filled with money. Mike probably put the tarps over them to keep out any moisture or dirt.

After all of the small-time cons and swindles that he'd

pulled, he had finally hit the big time.

Joe rushed forward, overcome with excitement, but stopped short when his lantern caught a drop-off in the shaft floor.

He swung the light back and forth to size up the situation.

There was another hole in the ground. This time, it stretched halfway across the passageway. If he stayed to the right, though, and bridged with his arms on the wall across from him, then he could shimmy to the other side.

Joe held the gun in one hand and the lantern in the other. He reached across to the wall and took the first step onto the narrow spit of ground on the right side of the hole.

As he touched the rock wall, he heard an ominous sound—a rattle and a hiss.

Joe pulled back and a large rattlesnake uncoiled in his direction. The snake aimed for the hand holding the lantern. Joe jerked, and the snake bit steel and glass.

Joe shone the lantern on the shelf that the snake had sat on, and he let loose with the gun.

The gunshots nearly deafened him, and the muzzle flashes lighted up the serpent on the rock.

Joe shone the lantern at the rock shelf. The snake lay dead. Caught in the light, he saw dead mice skeletons that littered the snake's nest. Mike must have been feeding this snake, thought Joe.

Joe got the involuntary shakes.

"Calm down, man. It's dead. You got him with the gun," he said to give himself confidence.

He thought about turning around and leaving with the wallet and the truck, but the prospect of the big haul was stronger than his fear of the hole or the snake.

Joe pressed on until he reached solid ground. He

breathed a sigh of relief and checked the ground in front of him. A slight breeze brushed Joe's face. The shaft must continue on until it comes to another opening, he thought. That must be how Mike had gotten the barrels in and out.

Joe made one last inspection of the ground in front of the money, and being satisfied, he rushed forward. The barrels were only about ten yards ahead, now. It looked to him that there might be four barrels under the tarp and two beside it. There was gold in the uncovered barrels, he was sure of it. At last, he thought, easy street was within his grasp.

Joe began to run. His right foot pushed him forward. His left foot landed and he tried to push off, but it sank into nothing.

He tried to back up, but it was too late—gravity pulled him forward. He tumbled, and dirt flew into the air around him. He thrust his arms above him hoping to find something to grab to save himself.

The light of his lantern turned skyward like a searchlight as he dropped down.

Joe felt the unmistakable feel of thick waxy tarp wrap around his body as he fell. Mike had covered a hole with a tarp and disguised it by sprinkling dirt over it. How long would it take to hit the bottom, he wondered? Would the hole be filled with water or jagged rocks?

He contemplated his end for but a brief second as he thudded onto solid ground, knocking the breath out of himself.

How lucky—he hadn't fallen into a bottomless pit, but only about eight to ten feet. If he hadn't broken or sprained anything, then he would probably be able to climb out.

Just as he started to feel better about his circumstances, he realized that he wasn't alone.

The lantern lay on his chest, and he picked it up and cast it frantically to and fro. The light caught dozens of serpentine shapes slithering all around him.

He felt them brush against his legs.

And then he felt them bite. They pierced his clothing and probed his body looking for any spot that they might strike. The white-hot puncture of their fangs repeatedly made his body cramp. He screamed out in panic to the emptiness.

After several horrifying minutes, he calmed down, and soon he no longer felt fear or pain. He only felt sleepy, weak, and cold.

Joe sensed the poison working on his respiration, his circulation, his faculties. His breathing became weak and ragged, and he had trouble thinking.

He'd fallen into a nest of rattlesnakes—of that he was sure. His worst nightmare had come true.

But, how? He'd been so careful. He had let his guard down in his excitement. Mike had gotten the last laugh.

Easy come, easy go, he thought—he had taken the risk and it hadn't paid off.

He could live with that—no wait, he corrected himself—he could *die* with that.

But, as he thought his last thoughts, and the rattlesnakes writhed and contorted around him—one question nagged him.

What about the rattles? Why hadn't he heard the rattlesnakes as he approached? Curious, he thought.

And then, as he took his last breath, he remembered Mike's necklace.

Made in the USA
Columbia, SC
08 September 2018